An

Affinity
for
Murder

An Affinity for Murder

Anne White

Oak Tree Press Claremont

Oak Tree Press

 For information, address Oak Tree Press, 915 West Foothill Boulevard, Suite 411, Claremont, CA 91711-3356.

Oak Tree Books may be purchased for educational, business, or sales promotion use. Contact Publisher for quantity discounts.

First Edition, July 2001

Cover Design by Yvet

Cover Art by Mary Montague Sikes

10 9 8 7 6 5 4 3 2 1

Library of Congress Cataloging-in-Publication Data
White, Anne
An Affinity for Murder/Anne White.
P. cm.
ISBN 1892343-16-9

1. Women Detectives—New York (State)—Lake George—Fiction. 2. O'Keeffe, Georgia, 1887-1986—Appreciation—Fiction. 3. Lake George (N.Y.) — Fiction. I. Title

PS3623.H57 A69 2001
813'.54—dc21 2001016406

An Affinity for Murder

A Lake George Mystery

Winner of the Dark Oak 2000
Mystery Contest

Winner of the 1999 Malice Domestic
Unpublished Writers' Grant

ACKNOWLEDGMENTS

I want to express my appreciation to:

Billie Johnson, publisher of Oak Tree Press, for naming An Affinity For Murder. A Lake George Mystery a winner in the Dark Oak 2000 Mystery Contest and for guiding it to publication.

Malice Domestic Limited for awarding me their Grant For Unpublished Writers in 1999.

John Strong and the Lake George Arts Project for their long series of outstanding writing programs and workshops.

With special thanks to:

Matt Witten who has always been willing to take time from his own busy writing schedule to be a helpful and generous mentor.

And to my daughter Kate White who has shared her expertise in writing, editing and publishing and given me unfailing encouragement and support.

AUTHOR'S NOTE

Although the characters and events in this novel are fictitious, Georgia O'Keeffe did spend summers from 1918 until the early 1930's at Lake George in upstate New York. While there, she drew inspiration from the lake and its environs to paint some of her best-loved masterpieces, including many of the large, erotic flower paintings often seen as her signature work. O'Keeffe enjoyed painting several versions of the same flower and — according to her biographers — destroyed those which did not meet her exacting standards. But what if remnants of this flower life had been left behind at Lake George and overlooked for more than seventy years?

After all, something very much like that had actually happened. In 1988, two years after O'Keeffe's death, twenty-eight paintings, which came to be known as the Canyon Suite, surfaced in Texas. Experts believed O'Keeffe had painted these watercolors between 1916 and 1918 when she was teaching in Canyon, Texas, and given them to a friend there. Authenticated by scholars, they were hailed as a national treasure and valued in the millions of dollars.

So, if O'Keeffe paintings could turn up in Texas, why not at Lake George as well? How this could happen struck me as a fascinating topic for a mystery, a fictitious account of the discovery of other long-lost paintings, which might or might not be O'Keeffe's work.

In late 1999, some time after I'd completed this book, experts associated with the National Gallery of Art determined that the twenty-eight Canyon Suite watercolors had not been painted by Georgia O'Keeffe and omitted them from the catalogue raisonne, or definitive catalog, of her work. What was not known at that time was the exact origin of these watercolors or how they came to be misattributed. The ongoing investigation into the real-life mystery of the Canyon Suite provides an unexpected counterpoint to this novel.

Anne White

ONE

If I'd known what October at Lake George held in store for me, I would have moved back to New York.

Or then again, maybe I wouldn't have.

Two hundred miles north of Manhattan the lakeshore around my uncle's cottage blazed with fall color so dazzling it stung my eyes to look at it. Psychedelic orange was the big shade that year and the wide swaths of it draped along the mountains on both sides of the lake reflected my mood to perfection. My romance with Kevin Mulvaney was heating up — and very nicely too, thank you — and, to send my mood spiking even higher, I'd come up with an idea for a feature article I felt sure would bring the New York Times beating on my door. Should I have suspected such good times couldn't last? Of course, but all that orange blindsided me.

My new friend, Diane Anderson, was as excited about my article as I was when I told her the topic over coffee one afternoon. "Georgia O'Keeffe at Lake George," she'd exclaimed. "Ellen, it's perfect. O'Keeffe's a twentieth century icon. She did some of her most beautiful paintings here and nobody outside the area seems to know it."

"So I'll tell 'em," I said.

"Right. Stir things up a little. Everyone associates her with New Mexico, especially now with the new museum in Santa Fe. It's high time we staked our claim to her too."

Diane, a mover and shaker in local arts organizations, was brimming over with ideas for me. "Edward Maranville's the man to start with," she said. "He knows absolutely everything about art. And right now he's staying at our summerhouse. I'll take you to meet him."

Although I'd met Diane only a few months before when I first moved to Lake George, we'd become friends quickly and I trusted her judgment. Sure, she tended to get a little bossy at times — a survival technique for anyone teaching high school students, I suspected — but most of her suggestions made sense. I told her to go ahead and set up an interview.

The following Sunday afternoon she picked me up at my uncle's camp, checked out my cassette recorder and note-taking materials in her teacherly fashion and drove me north along the lake. A few miles beyond Lake George Village she turned down a side road and pointed out the summer cottage she still owned jointly with her ex-husband. I could see why neither had been willing to sell out to the other. The white bungalow with its broad front porch and spectacular view of the lake looked like an ideal vacation retreat — except there was something wrong with the picture. As we pulled into the driveway, we smelled the unmistakable odor of smoke, sharp and acrid, coming from the cottage.

"Oh God. Edward's been careless about the fireplace." Diane jumped out of the car and ran toward the porch. She took the steps two at a time and banged open the front door. I crowded in behind her.

The fireplace wasn't the problem. Even with my eyes watering from the thick, foul smelling smoke, I could see that. A fire was smoldering in the middle of the living room floor in a charred pile of blankets and other bedding.

"Fire extinguisher?" I yelled. When I didn't see one hanging anywhere, I ran to the kitchen and yanked open cupboard doors until I found a good-sized pot. I filled it with water and stuck another pan under the faucet while I rushed into the living room and emptied the first one on the fire.

As I raced back to the kitchen, Diane reached into a broom closet and pulled out a fire extinguisher. I dumped my second pan of water, then stepped back while she sprayed foam over the soggy mess on the floor. She leaned down and pulled aside some of the larger pieces of blanket and sprayed again. The stench from the fire was sickening. We were both coughing and gagging. Even with one hand clamped over my nose, I couldn't shut out the vile smell.

Diane shook her head in bewilderment. "Somebody set this fire deliberately, didn't they? They've taken stuff out of our linen closet — the extra bedspreads, our new blankets. This is arson, isn't it?"

It sure looked like it to me. I lifted hunks of the wet bedding and dropped them into the pans. "We'd better check the floorboards, make sure nothing's smoldering underneath."

"All right, but give me a minute." Diane cradled her hand and disappeared into a downstairs bathroom.

I flicked at the pile, separating the half-burned fragments of blue and green wool. Suddenly, the floorboards were the least of my concerns. My fingers brushed across a large, firm object, something that felt suspiciously like an arm. I swept more pieces of blanket aside. Under the bedding at the bottom of the pile I could see what looked like a heap of scorched clothing. But it wasn't a heap of clothing.

The partially burned body of a man lay on his side facing away from me. The handle of a long, thin knife or letter opener protruded from his back. Blood had puddled up around the wound and formed a grotesque strawberry mark on the man's tweed sport coat. The smell coming from the body and from the singed hair was sickening enough but it was the face, when I leaned sideways to look at it, that really started my stomach churning. I'd never seen anything like that face. It lay half-hidden against the carpet, a repulsive lump of flesh, charred as black as a piece of meat seared on a grill.

I sat back hard on my heels and let out a frightened yelp. "Diane, come quick."

Diane hurried out of the bathroom, squeezing a tube of ointment over her hand. She gasped when she saw the body. "Oh God. Is it Edward?"

"I don't know. I never saw Edward. You have to tell me."

She moved closer, inching forward with the smallest possible steps until she could see the face. "How could this have happened? Did someone kill him?"

"Diane, someone must have." Was she in shock? I wondered. The guy couldn't have looked more dead. Plus he had a knife sticking out of him. But maybe... I reached for his left hand — his right one looked like a black leather glove some kid had stuffed for Halloween — and tried to find a pulse. The hand felt like a fake hand, cold and smooth and totally lifeless.

My stomach responded with a violent flip. I thought I was going to throw up, but I gritted my teeth and held onto the wrist until I was sure there was no flicker of life. Then I stood up fast and backed away from the body. "Where's your phone? We've got to call for help, get the sheriff up here and the rescue squad too, although it looks like it's too late for them."

I waited, expecting Diane to make the calls, but she slumped against the wall, motionless as if she'd taken root there. She kept one hand pressed against her nose and mouth and waved the other at a white telephone on a little maple stand near the door to the kitchen. I went over and picked up the phone. Fingerprints were the last thing on my mind. I wanted only to summon help -- sheriff's deputies, rescue squad, fire department, anybody linked by invisible strands to the omnipotent 9-1-1 emergency number. There was no dial tone. The telephone was as dead as the man on the floor.

"Somebody killed him. Why?" Diane's voice was so weak I could hardly hear her. "He called me last week and I told him he could stay here. John was annoyed. I didn't understand it. He's let him use this place other times."

"John? Your ex-husband?"

She didn't answer, just stared at me wide-eyed as if she was spacing out.

"Let's not worry about that now," I said with more sharpness than I intended. "We've got to go somewhere and call the sheriff."

Diane leaned forward and peered down at the body again, then collapsed back against the wall, her face ashen.

I went to her and put my arm around her shoulders. "You look like you're going to faint. You'd better get some fresh air." I guided her into the hall and opened the front door for her.

I was starting to follow her outside when I stopped and took one last look back into the living room. The smoke had cleared enough for me to notice something that hadn't registered before. Every light in the room was turned on — an overhead fixture, three reading lamps turned up as bright as they would go, a small, decorative lamp with a surprisingly high-powered bulb. Even with the tendrils of smoke hanging in the air, the room looked like a badly lit stage. Neither Diane nor I had turned lights on when we came in. Could they have been left on since last night? Had the murder taken place then?

As I stood in the archway, I caught a flash of movement out of the corner of my eye. The hall was dark compared to the over-bright living room, too dark for me to see who came bounding down the stairs behind me. I felt a glancing blow to my head and then two big hands slammed hard against my back. I caught a whiff of something I didn't recognize just before I pitched headfirst into the living room, lurching out of control, clutching fistfuls of air as I flailed about, grabbing for anything that would break my fall. I fought to stay on my feet; I didn't want to fall on top of the dead man. I could see myself landing on him, driving that knife even deeper into his back as the murderer drove another one into mine. I got hold of a small table. It tilted and skittered away from me until, after what seemed an eternity, the far edge struck a chair and it steadied just long enough to stop me from crashing into the brick fireplace. I ended up sprawled on the hearth slates, listening to cries of protest from a dozen places on my body. My right knee shrieked like a banshee but I rolled over fast and grabbed one of the brass fireplace tools. I got my good knee under me and raised myself up as much as I could. I brandished the poker, ready to defend myself against the figure barreling down on me. I thought it was my attacker coming to finish me off. To my relief, I saw Diane heading toward me.

"Ellen, what happened?"

"Somebody ran down the stairs and out the back door. Look. Quick."

Diane hurried to the kitchen window and peered out, even fastened the chain on the back door and opened it a crack for a cautious look-around, but she was too late. Whoever it was had disappeared. She slammed the door hard and turned the key in the lock.

By the time she came back into the living room, I'd gotten myself into a sitting position. I ran my hands cautiously over my kneecaps. No cracks, no dents, but my right knee throbbed with pain. "Diane, give me a hand up, will you?" I said.

Diane took hold of both my hands and pulled me to my feet. I knew I was dead weight but I couldn't help it.

"Can you walk?" she asked.

I stepped forward gingerly, testing my knee. It hurt even more when I put weight on my foot, but it didn't buckle. "I'm okay."

"The murderer must have been hiding upstairs all the time. What if he's waiting for us outside?" she said.

"I don't want to be trapped in here without a phone. We've got to make a run for your car," I told her.

"Oh Ellen, I'm so sorry you got hurt. Can you ever forgive me for dragging you into this?"

I made a little brushing movement with my hand and let it pass for an answer. I really didn't think Diane could be blamed for anything that had happened — at least I didn't think so right then -- but with my stomach doing flip-flops and my knee burning like hellfire, that little brushing motion was the best I could manage.

TWO

Diane and I cracked the front door a few inches at a time and did a thorough check of the area around the cottage. When we were finally satisfied no one was lying in wait for us, we ran for the car, both of us darting anxious looks back over our shoulders toward the woods behind us. Neither of us saw anyone but I swore I could feel the murderer's eyes boring into me from behind a tree.

As we raced up the road toward the highway, I stared out the car window at the cottages we passed, watching for cars, chimney smoke, anything to indicate that someone might have stayed on this late in the year. There were no signs of life.

Diane gripped the wheel so hard her fingers bleached out white as her face. The red blister on the back of her hand puffed up, shiny and painful looking. Suddenly, she cut sharply to the right and we plunged onto an even narrower road that threaded its way through a stand of scruffy pine trees. "Hang on. This is a short cut."

We bounced through ruts, zigzagged around outcroppings of rock and slammed to a stop in a paved parking area. I did a double take. Ahead of us loomed a Tudor mansion straight off the cover of a Gothic romance, an architectural extravaganza from another time, complete with half-timbered walls, mullioned windows and a magnificent stone terrace overlooking the lake.

"Diane, what is this place?" I asked

She pointed at a small discreet sign — Marlborough House Inn.

When you owned something this impressive, you apparently didn't need a big sign.

"Come on. We can use the phone here." Diane, her voice still shaky, slid out of the car. After one quick glance to make sure I was behind her, she ran across the well-tended expanse of lawn, up a flight of stone steps to the terrace and down a smaller stairway on the other side. I didn't ask questions, just hobbled after her as fast as I could. As we hit the edge of the grassy slope bordering the lake, she veered through a basement-level door into a kind of rathskeller.

The room was empty except for a big, good-looking guy lounging behind the bar, watching a football game on TV. Probably the New York Giants, a team much loved in this part of the world, I'd discovered.

The minute the bartender saw us he jumped up and hurried out from behind the bar. They did a great job with men around here; I had to concede that. This guy came complete with thick dark hair and a body that wouldn't have been out of place on a beefcake calendar. If Brooks Brothers had known how sexy he made a white dress shirt look, they would have used him in their advertising.

"Diane, what is it?" The man lifted his arms as if he wanted to reach out to her, but dropped them quickly.

Diane began to describe the scene we'd stumbled

on, then stopped short to tell me, "Ellen, this is Tom Durocher, a former student of mine."

Before Tom and I could do anything more than nod at each other, she launched into an explanation of why Edward Maranville had been staying at her summer-house.

Tom interrupted her. "Hold on a minute, Diane. Let me get the sheriff and the rescue squad over there and then you can tell me the rest." He turned away from us and picked up a phone on the counter behind the bar.

So he not only looked studly, he could handle an emergency. I didn't hear much of what he said, but I watched him, trying to figure how he could have been Diane's student when they appeared so close to the same age. Maybe teaching high school English had advantages I'd never considered.

Several minutes passed, punctuated by long silences, while Tom with the phone to his ear paced back and forth behind the bar as far as the cord would reach. He finally hung up and walked over to us. "They said you should wait right here. A sheriff's investigator will come over to take your statements."

"Oh great. Just my luck they'll send Jack Whittemore," Diane said.

"Can't be helped. You have to make a statement. You too, Ellen." Tom pointed us toward a little table near the bar.

Diane collapsed in a chair, her face deathly white against her auburn hair. The freckles across her nose and cheeks stood out like spatters of paint flicked on with a brush. She lifted her hand to show Tom her burn and he rummaged through a drawer until he found a tube of ointment.

As she rambled on about finding Edward's body, Diane rubbed the ointment around and around her burn, talking steadily, slip-sliding from one subject to another as if her mind were spinning in circles too. "It was awful seeing Edward that way, burned so bad. I'm the one who said he could stay there. John didn't want him there this year. He's the one told him he could stay there other times when I was against it. I thought Edward had just called me as a courtesy. I guess I should have been more suspicious."

Tom and I exchanged concerned glances. "You both could use a drink," he said. He pulled out a bottle of white wine, filled two glasses to the brim and brought them to our table.

Diane couldn't seem to stop talking. Tom and I both cast around for ways to divert her, but she wasn't hearing us. "Edward's a client of John's, you know. John doesn't like to refuse a client but he wanted me to refuse him. That's the way he does things." Her torrent of words continued non-stop.

A heavy-set man with a shock of sandy hair suddenly materialized at the far end of the bar. Tom excused himself and walked down to him. The man muttered "the usual" with a slight accent I couldn't place, then drummed his fingers on the bar as Tom poured a very large Scotch rocks and set it in front of him. Tom leaned forward and said something in a low voice. The man shook his head. He muttered a few words to Tom, then gulped down his drink and left.

I swung my chair around and stared out the big side windows of the bar toward the Anderson cottage, trying to shut out Diane's voice as she went on and on about Edward.

"Why isn't anybody over there yet?" I demanded but, of course, neither Tom or Diane had an answer for me.

It was almost dark before we heard the distant whine of sirens echoing from the highway and saw the first flashing red lights through the trees. As we watched an ambulance, two fire trucks and several sheriff's vehicles jockey for position in the Andersons' yard, Diane bent forward over the table, wrapping her arms around herself, trembling uncontrollably.

"You're freezing, Diane," Tom said. "I'd better get a fire going. Who knows how long it'll take for an investigator to get over here." He went into the hall at the far end of the bar and called to someone.

In a few minutes a tall, lanky teenager dragged in a canvas carryall loaded with wood. Without glancing in our direction, he began cramming a mismatched assortment of logs into the metal cradle in the bar's huge stone fireplace.

Watching the boy proved a temporary antidote to the gloom settling over me. I'd acquired my own personal fire starter recently, Kevin Mulvaney, an environmental analyst I'd met my first morning at Lake George. Comparing this kid's slapdash style with Kevin's fire-building technique got my mind off the murder, at least temporarily. A few weeks into our friendship, Kevin had uncovered a fireplace hidden behind paneling in my uncle's living room and had taken to dropping by on nippy fall nights to build fires for me. The man built a fire the same way he did everything else — slowly, methodically and with such pleasing attention to detail I usually started remembering how he employed those same skills in other activities and invited him to spend the night.

The boy struggled for another ten minutes before the flames leapt up enough for him to add the last of the logs. When he finally got to his feet and turned to go, Diane recognized him.

"Billy, I didn't realize that was you," she said.

"Hi, Miz Anderson." The boy shifted from one foot to another, obviously at a loss for anything more to say.

Tom came to his rescue. "Thanks, Bill. Better get back to the kitchen before they come looking for you."

"Billy's in my English 10 class this year," Diane told Tom and me after the boy had left. "His dad got laid off at one of the mills a few months ago. Big family. I'm glad to see Bill's got a job here."

Tom brought over the bottle of Chardonnay. I

glanced toward Diane. Seeing Billy had gotten her off the subject of Edward, but she was definitely too frazzled to drink any more. I shook my head at Tom but, if he noticed, he didn't let on. He refilled our glasses and ambled back behind the bar.

I shoved my glass away and jumped up, as agitated as if I'd done the murder myself and was waiting for the sheriff to come and cart me off to jail. I went over to a window and pressed my forehead against the icy pane but by this time all I could see was blackness broken only by the steady flashing of red and blue lights beyond the screen of trees.

Something in the far corner of the bar caught my eye. Hanging on the wall was a Georgia O'Keeffe painting I'd seen at the Museum of Modern Art. Of course, this was only a copy, a poster really, in a thin metal frame but I stopped to look. The colors weren't quite true to the original's but the soft shades of green and the horizontal lines of the shutters and clapboards still held their familiar appeal for me.

"Tom, I love this Georgia O'Keeffe," I said.

Tom switched on the track lights along the wall to give me a better look. "Do you know that one? It's called Lake George Window. The inn's owners have some other prints of hers hanging upstairs. Her husband's family lived right up the road. O'Keeffe spent summers here for a long time."

"I know. I plan to do some writing about her and the time she spent here. In fact, that's why we went to Diane's place today. I was going to interview Edward Maranville about her."

Tom nodded. "He would have been a good one to talk to, all right. He and those friends of his who stayed here were always yakking about her and the Stieglitz family. Like they knew 'em personally."

His remark got Diane's attention. "Edward had friends who stayed here? What friends?" she asked him.

"Artsy friends, city people. That was one of 'em came in a few minutes ago. He'd heard the news about Edward. He was so upset he could hardly talk," Tom said.

"Do they stay here often? Funny I've never heard Edward mention them."

"They keep rooms here at the inn. Most nights when they're around, Edward comes in and has drinks with them, talks art and art collecting. Or I guess I should say that's what he used to do."

"And they talked a lot about Georgia O'Keeffe?" I asked.

"Nuts about her. Went ape over the fact she'd spent summers near here. I never understood half of what they said even when they didn't have their heads together whispering."

"Whispering? Why would they whisper about her?" I asked.

Before Tom could answer, an ambulance pulled out of Diane's yard and went careening up the road toward the highway. My stomach lurched as I thought of the man inside. Why were they driving so fast when it was too late?

Diane watched the lights of the ambulance disappear, her eyes filling. "Edward used to say he didn't want people looking at him when he was dead. Every time I saw him after he'd been to a wake, he'd tell me that." The last words caught in her throat and turned into a sob. She laid her head on her arms, no longer able to hold back her tears.

I patted her shoulder and made the soothing noises you make when you're trying to comfort someone. Tom, looking awkward, shoved a pile of cocktail napkins toward her. Diane's sobs grew louder, interspersed with moans and hiccups. She wadded up the napkins and held them to her mouth, as if they could muffle the awful sounds pouring out it. She was into major falling apart, in no shape to make a statement to a sheriff's investigator or anybody else. Her wineglass and mine were both empty now. I shot Tom a questioning glance but, once again, he pretended not to notice.

"Tom, could you get us some coffee?" I asked.

He picked up the phone to call the kitchen but, before he could do it, things went spinning faster and farther out of control. Sheriff's Investigator Jack Whittemore, the last person in the world Diane should talk to without all her wits about her, came striding through the door.

Jack didn't wear the dark gray uniform and wide-brimmed gray hat of the local sheriff's department but even in his navy blazer and khakis, he was a formidable sight. Well over six feet tall, barrel-chested, with arms and legs like small tree trunks, he bore down on the table where Diane and I were sitting. He didn't soften his image by smiling. "Diane Anderson. Ellen Davies. I need to get statements from you both."

The investigator stared first at Diane's ravaged face, then at the empty wineglasses still on the table. He glared his disapproval. "I'll start with you, Mrs. Anderson. Will you come with me, please."

THREE

"Jack'll have a field day with her the state she's in," Tom muttered as we watched Jack Whittemore and a sheriff's deputy escort Diane out of the bar.

"I was thinking the same thing," I admitted. "I had an experience with that man when I first moved to the lake. He can get you to where you don't know if you're coming or going faster than anyone I ever saw, even when you're clearheaded. And Diane is anything but that."

Tom shook his head sympathetically. "She's pretty strung out, all right. She's been in bad shape ever since the divorce. Now she'll have all this to deal with."

I knew enough about Diane's life before I met her to fill in some of the blanks. She'd been married to John Anderson, a successful CPA, for almost two decades when the year before, out of the blue, he'd asked her for a divorce. True, he'd never spent much time at home, claimed to be working late most nights, but she'd figured him for a workaholic. They had one son, in high school by then, and English teachers always have papers to correct so she was busy enough not to complain about her husband's work habits. On weekends she and John kept up an active social life and she'd never suspected that on those weeknights when she thought he was slaving over his spreadsheets he'd been spending his time on a different kind of sheets entirely, silk probably, since he'd taken up with the daughter of the town's wealthiest family — Sydney Vanderhoff.

Tom may have been too quick with the wine, but he was right about one thing: Diane didn't need any more problems in her life. I'd started to agree with him when I realized he'd disappeared. He returned a few minutes later carrying a carafe of coffee.

"Too bad we didn't have this sooner," I said as he filled a mug and handed it to me. So I sounded like an ingrate — I didn't care.

"You mean for Diane? It's not too late. I can take her some."

To my surprise, he filled another mug with coffee, added cream and sugar just the way Diane liked it and carried it out of the bar.

I drained my mug and reached for the carafe to pour myself a refill. I couldn't remember when anything had tasted as good as that coffee. By the time I finished it, I'd stopped obsessing about Diane's mental state and was concentrating on finding something to think about besides the murder. I glanced over at the Lake George Window print. My article. If I could just think about what to do next...

The article was important to me; I wasn't about to give up on it. A few months earlier when I talked my uncle into letting me use his rustic camp as a temporary writer's retreat, I thought I'd found the perfect spot to finish the book of career advice I'd been working on for the past year. No neighbors, no interruptions, I'd told myself. I'd wrap up the book fast, then head back to New York. Except things hadn't worked out quite the way I planned.

My very first week at the lake, I was hit over the head by a powerful economic truth -- savings disappear quickly when there's no income to supplement them. Freelancing for the local newspaper didn't pay much and cut down on the time I could spend on the book, but the occasional feature article I'd been writing for the Post Standard helped me squeak by financially. Now with a little experience under my belt, I could set my sights on higher paying outlets, maybe even the New York papers.

Poor dead Edward Maranville wouldn't be giving interviews on Georgia O'Keeffe or anyone else, but there had to be other people I could talk to. After all, O'Keeffe was a world-class artist. And Diane was right – some of her best-loved masterpieces, including many of her gigantic flower paintings, had been painted during her fifteen summers at Lake George. Tom had mentioned that the inn's owners liked her work. Maybe I could talk to them.

I heard voices and saw Tom returning without the mug of coffee. "Somebody's here looking for you, Ellen," he said.

Kevin Mulvaney followed Tom into the bar. The minute he came through the door, I felt the familiar rat-a-tat-tat in my insides his appearance always triggered. I'd met Kevin my first day at the lake when he'd arrived at my uncle's camp with a team of divers to check out something with the unlikely name, benthic barriers. These were mats, he'd explained, that his watchdog environmental agency laid on the floor of the lake to retard the growth of Eurasian milfoil, a pesky aquatic weed. That morning Kevin had told me a little more about milfoil and its devastating effect on lakes than I really wanted to know, but all the time he talked, he kept zinging me with powerful pheromones that added a surprising sexual underlay to our conversation. And, as if sudden, overwhelming physical attraction to a complete stranger wouldn't have been enough to mess up my new life all by itself, his craggy good looks and quiet strength put me in mind of childhood heroes like Hawkeye and Rogers' Rangers who'd played such romantic roles in the lake's past. Right from the first, I was smitten, and it was the last thing in the world I wanted to be.

As Kevin hurried across the bar toward me that Sunday evening, his tan slacks and jacket — not buckskin of course but close enough — and his new style wire- rimmed glasses didn't detract at all from his frontiersman image. "Ellen, are you all right?" he asked anxiously.

I liked his concern. "I'm okay. How did you find out I was here?"

"One of the guys on the rescue squad gave me the news. He said Edward Maranville had been found dead and you were involved."

"Involved? I wasn't involved. I found his body, that's all, and believe me, it wasn't anything I wanted to do." I'd set a new record — from being relieved to see him to snapping at him in two seconds flat. I was an innocent victim of circumstances here, wasn't I? Why would he think anything else?

He leaned over and kissed me on the cheek. "Look, I know you've had a tough day. I heard Maranville's body was badly burned. Was it awful finding him like that?"

Sympathy seemed preferable to an argument, so I climbed down off my high horse. "His face and one hand were burned black. It's hard to stop thinking about him."

Tom wandered toward us. "Beer, Kevin?"

"I'd better not. I've got a meeting tomorrow to prepare for. I'll take some of that coffee though if there's any left." Kevin sat down across from me at the little table.

I really was glad to see him. I leaned back in my

chair, feeling the tension in my shoulders drain away. I could manage perfectly all right without a protective male at my side, but there was something reassuring about having an ally, especially one with Kevin's common sense. I couldn't imagine him letting Diane load up on wine the way Tom had done.

"So start at the beginning. Tell me everything that happened," Kevin said.

That was exactly what I wanted to do. The guy was a great listener. He'd honed his listening skills as director of the Lake Protection Group, hearing out a steady stream of individuals and factions with conflicting opinions on the lake's economic and environmental concerns. I'd pegged him immediately as a scientific/investigative type on the Holland codes, if you'll pardon a little of the career counseling terminology I used in my New York job. When Kevin listened, I got the feeling a Pentium chip was clicking away in his brain, sorting and analyzing data.

"You said you were going to interview Edward Maranville about Georgia O'Keeffe. So start there."

Tom didn't give me a chance to start. "Those two were pretty spooked when they got here," he said as he handed Kevin a mug of coffee.

"Hey, you would be too if you thought you'd stumbled on a case of arson and it turned out to be murder," I told him.

"Yeah. Somebody set the place on fire," Tom went on. "That's why the fire company's been there. I think they're still there. Must be they're not sure it's out yet."

"You knew right away the cottage was on fire?" Kevin asked me.

"Not really, but there was a lot of smoke. Diane thought Edward had been careless with the fireplace."

"Sure you don't want a beer, Kevin?" Tom said.

Kevin shook his head without looking at him. "Go on, Ellen. You saw the smoke but you opened the front door anyway?"

I almost made a crack about hindsight being a great gift but stopped myself in time. "As I said, Diane thought something had gone wrong with the fireplace. We didn't expect to find a fire smoldering in the middle of the living room floor, you know."

"Diane got quite a burn on her hand," Tom said.

Kevin clenched his teeth. A muscle twitched along his jaw. "Ellen, go on. You tried to put out the fire?"

"We did put it out. I wanted to see if it had burned into the floorboards so I shoved some of the blankets aside. I touched something and it was an arm." Suddenly, I could feel that cold, lifeless flesh again. I was going to be sick.

"They both looked pretty strung out when they got here," Tom said.

Kevin tossed a quick glance in Tom's direction and got to his feet. "You'd better get some fresh air, Ellen. We can stand outside while you wait for Jack."

"She's supposed to wait here," Tom said.

"We'll be right outside the door. You'll be here. Tell him Ellen needed some air."

I headed out, ready to compliment Kevin on his problem-solving ability, but we were too late. Jack Whittemore appeared at the far door, motioning to me.

"You'd better go home. This may take a while," I whispered to Kevin.

"Why don't I wait and see how it goes? I don't mind."

I shook my head. Jack was tough, but I could handle him.

At least I thought I could. Before Kevin was out the door, I was having second thoughts. Diane had followed Jack into the bar, looking like a character in an Anne Rice novel who'd been drained of her life blood. She actually staggered on her way back to the table and dropped into her chair without a word. Hardly a reassuring sight for the investigator's next victim.

FOUR

The investigator and a deputy waited for me near the door to the hall. Jack Whittemore's annoyed glance at the television where the Giants were making a desperate fourth quarter stand revealed his unhappiness with the way his day had gone. It was almost seven o'clock. Either the Giants were playing on the West Coast or he was missing the longest football game in history.

Halfway down the hall, he opened the door to a small room and indicated that I was to go in. "We can talk privately here," he said, glaring at me as if I were the one responsible for lousing up his Sunday.

The room he'd chosen seemed intended for nothing except storage. Chairs were scattered about at odd angles; dressers and other pieces of furniture were pushed back against the walls. He motioned me to a chair that had been pulled up to a small table and sat down opposite me.

Once we were settled, the investigator produced a small beige notebook and wrote my name on the top of a blank page. He asked if I was still staying at my uncle's place at the cove and, when I nodded, wrote the name Ray Harron in parentheses next to mine. Ray had been living in Hague farther up the lake for years but he was still considered a Lake George native. I wasn't a native but I got minor credit for having spent summers as a child with Ray and my aunt Mattie. I volunteered that I'd had a telephone installed in the camp and gave him my number.

"So you're planning to stay on for a while?" he asked, sounding less than pleased with the possibility. Xenophobia seemed to be a common condition among the males I'd been meeting at the lake. Either that or there was something about my city ways that annoyed the hell out of them.

Retorts popped into my mind, but I kept my mouth shut. All I wanted was to get out of the Marlborough House Inn and home to my peaceful little cottage on the cove. Besides, I'd suddenly realized I was ravenously hungry.

"Go ahead, Investigator. Let's get this over with. Interrogate me."

"Ms. Davies," he said scornfully, "what I am about to do is interview you. If you were a suspect, then I would interrogate you. There's a difference."

"That's good news," I said. My nervousness had turned me into a smart-mouth. I gave my arm a pinch.

"Mrs. Anderson told me you accompanied her to her summerhouse. You planned to conduct some kind of interview with Mr. Maranville for an article you're writing?"

"Right." I still sounded smart-alecky. Another pinch. I wasn't trying to annoy this man, was I?

"Mrs. Anderson had arranged for you to talk with him?"

"I believe so, yes."

His head jerked up as if I'd struck him. "You're not sure whether she'd arranged the meeting or not?"

The question put me on the defensive, but I took a deep breath and tried to keep my cool. "She'd agreed to call him. I assumed she had. I can't swear to it."

"So, earlier that afternoon, Mrs. Anderson picked you up and drove you to her summerhouse to meet with Mr. Maranville. Did you see anyone else as you drove in? Did you notice a car or truck parked anywhere nearby?"

"No, but I really wasn't looking for one. Besides, there are many places in those woods where someone could park a car and not be seen."

"You didn't hear or see anything out of the ordinary?"

"No. Not until we got to Diane's and saw the smoke." I described how we'd rushed into the cottage and put out the fire.

"You were in the room with Mrs. Anderson when she found the body?"

Had Diane told him she found the body or was Whittemore trying to trick me? I wasn't going to play games. "I'm the one who found the body. Diane had gone into the bathroom to get ointment for a burn on her hand. I pushed the blankets around to make sure the fire was out — and I felt the body underneath them."

"Yes. All right. What did you do then?"

"I shouted to Diane and she came right out."

"Did you notice burned matches or newspapers, a cigarette lighter, anything that might have been used to start the fire?"

"No."

"Were you aware that no accelerant had been used, no gasoline or kerosene, nothing like that?"

"No."

He frowned. "Ms. Davies, I need you to tell me as much as you possibly can. Don't leave out any detail even if it doesn't seem important to you. Let me be the one to decide what's relevant."

"No. I didn't see matches or papers or anything like that. And I never thought about how the fire had been started. We were only thinking about putting it out."

"All right. You've found the body. How did you know the man was dead?"

"I really didn't know for sure, I guess. Edward looked dead and there was that awful smell." God, I'd never even met the poor devil and I'd put him on a first name basis.

"So what did you do then?"

"I tried to get a pulse."

"It was you who checked his pulse, not Mrs. Anderson?"

Had I done the wrong thing? Did I somehow contaminate the crime scene? "Look, I felt I had to. I took care not to disturb anything."

The questions went on and on — questions about the fire, the bedding pulled from the linen closet, the dead phone.

I answered as accurately and with as much detail as I could. No more Ms. Smart Mouth for me. Whether this was an interview or an interrogation, I wanted to get it over with.

When the investigator launched into questions about the man who pushed me, I began to stumble over my answers. He pressured me for details on how and when I'd become aware of someone on the stairs, on what I'd seen or heard when the intruder rushed at me. So much of it was a blur, but his last question triggered a small, indefinable memory. I'd smelled something for a second, something different from the awful smell already permeating the room, not a scent, not an unpleasant odor, something homey and warm I couldn't quite describe, a food smell maybe. I really couldn't say what it was. I started to mention it, then foresaw a string of questions I wouldn't be able to answer and decided to skip it.

When Jack Whittemore was finally satisfied he'd

picked my brain clean about the man who pushed me, he checked back to the beginning of his notes and reviewed what I'd told him. "Bear with me on this, Ms. Davies. I want to be sure I haven't misunderstood anything."

Several times he returned to a subject which seemed to puzzle him — the brightly-lighted room. "You're sure the lights were all turned on when you came in? You don't think Mrs. Anderson might have switched on the overhead light as she came through the door?"

"I know she didn't. It was still daylight when we got there. And it wasn't just that the lights were turned on. They were so bright. Not the way a room would be lighted ordinarily."

Finally, he paused and I asked the question uppermost in my mind, even though I wasn't at all sure I wanted to know the answer. "So, do you think the man who ran down the stairs and shoved me was the murderer?"

"Do you?" Always the detective. Ask, don't tell.

"But why would he hang around if he'd already set the place on fire?" I said.

"Good question. And I don't have an answer for it. Are you acquainted with Mrs. Anderson's ex-husband?"

"What?" It took me a minute to get back up to speed. "No. I know who he is, that's all."

"John Anderson of Anderson, Lowell Accounting?"

"I don't think I ever heard the name of his firm, but I guess that must be it."

"And you know he and Mrs. Anderson share ownership of their summerhouse?"

"She told me that, yes."

"And did she tell you how Mr. Maranville happened to be staying there?"

Now, we were getting to the tricky part. I wasn't about to mention any disagreements between them.

"He's their friend. I believe he's stayed at their place other times."

"When she offered to arrange an interview for you, that seemed plausible to you?"

"Yes. Of course."

"But you don't know for sure if she actually arranged it?"

"No. But I assumed she did."

"You have your own car, don't you?"

"Yes. I do."

"And yet it seemed plausible that Mrs. Anderson would bring you to meet Mr. Maranville and sit in on your interview?"

"Yes."

He tapped his pen on the table, frowning as if he didn't know what to make of this information but saying nothing.

When I couldn't stand the silence any longer, I asked, "Are you implying Diane expected to find something wrong and didn't want to come up here alone?"

He closed his notebook and stood up. "I'm not implying anything, Ms. Davies. I make every effort to say exactly what I mean. Please don't read anything more into it. Now, I'll say exactly what I mean on another matter." He paused — for dramatic effect, I guess -- and looked down at me with his signature scowl. "Mrs. Anderson has had much too much to drink. She lives in Glens Falls and should not attempt to drive that ten miles herself. I want you to insist on driving her and make sure she gets home all right. Otherwise, I'll have to send a deputy to do it."

FIVE

The last thing in the world I wanted to do that night was drive Diane back to Glens Falls, but Jack Whittemore was right — she was in no condition to drive herself. When I returned to the bar, I found her sitting on a stool across from Tom. She was still close to hysteria, crying and talking non-stop about the murder. I suspected she'd drunk more wine while I was gone but I suppose she could have been in some kind of shock. She'd known the murdered man pretty well, after all. I hadn't known him at all and I kept seeing his blackened face and hand and that knife sticking out of his ribs when I least expected it.

"We can leave now, Diane. I'll drive you home," I said.

Tom nodded his approval. Jack Whittemore stood just inside the hall door, watching, apparently ready to make good on his promise to send a deputy if she didn't agree.

I'd anticipated an argument but, to my relief, Diane didn't protest. She handed me her keys right then and there and, when we reached her car, climbed into the passenger seat without comment. I looked for Kevin's car, hoping he might have decided to hang around after all, but it wasn't there.

Diane leaned her head back against the seat and took a deep, ragged breath. I expected another rush of talk but she didn't say a word. She didn't even comment when I stopped by my uncle's and we exchanged her car for my van. At least, I'd have my own transportation. Diane could get by without her car for the night anyway.

My original plan to drop her off and drive right back to the lake didn't work out any better than anything else had that day. When we got to her condo -- the house she'd shared with John had been sold months ago, she told me, and that prompted a fresh rush of tears -- she begged me to come in for a few minutes. Once I did, I was stuck.

As soon as she'd unlocked the front door, Diane made a beeline for the telephone. "I'm calling the Teachers' Registry to arrange for a substitute. There's no way I can go to school tomorrow."

"Smart move," I said. I waited until she'd dialed the number, then took the phone from her. At this hour she'd be talking to a tape but whoever listened to it in the morning couldn't miss noticing the slur in her voice.

She coached me with the necessary information then disappeared into the kitchen. As soon as I got off the phone, she called, "How about scrambled eggs?"

I couldn't resist the offer. The scrambled eggs and the bagels we toasted to go with them tasted like gourmet fare, but the minute I finished eating a rush of fatigue overwhelmed me and my eyelids started drooping right there at Diane's kitchen table.

"Ellen, please stay here tonight," she pleaded for the fifth or sixth time. "I'm all alone now with Jonathan away at school. It'll mean so much to have you here."

I'd said no when she'd asked before but this time I was too sleepy to refuse. I accepted the invitation.

Diane found me a washcloth and towel and an oversized tee shirt to wear for a nightgown and showed me to her son's room. It was a perfect boy's bedroom -- sheets and comforter in an attractive gray and brown geometric print, an old fashioned rolltop desk and an interesting looking book collection I would have checked out if I hadn't been so tired. Maybe in the morning if I woke up early, I promised myself, and snuggled down under the covers.

I'd expected to be out the minute my head hit the pillow but somehow sleep slithered away from me every time I came close to it. How had I gotten into this mess, I kept asking myself. The day had started on such a positive note; I couldn't believe it had ended so badly. And yet so many of my days had ended unhappily recently. Was I doing something to cause these downswings, something I wasn't even aware of?

And what about Diane? I'd met her through another new friend, Kate Donohue, shortly after I arrived in Lake George. Kate and I had hit it off immediately, but Kate, a single parent committed to moving her two-year-old catering business into the black, had little free time for socializing. So she'd insisted on bringing Diane and me together. "You two will like each other," she'd predicted and she was right.

Diane and I both loved rattling on about books and films and were usually on the same page in our assessments of them, disagreeing just often enough to keep our discussions lively. We'd begun meeting for coffee or an occasional lunch at Kate's little restaurant and I'd quickly come to see Diane as a friend too. But it was more than our shared enthusiasm for books and movies that drew us together.

Diane had a quick wit and a wry approach to life I found appealing. We were both needy, but neither of us wanted to belabor that point. Diane had lost husband, home and friends in the divorce. Bad enough. Then, while she was still reeling from those losses, her son Jonathan, devastated by the break-up of his parents' marriage, had opted for private school. Except for school vacations and an occasional weekend, she was alone. Yet, despite all this she came across as a resilient person. She understood better than most what it had meant to me to exchange my comfortable life in Manhattan for a less than glamorous existence in my uncle's rundown little camp.

"We're both starting over, like Burt Reynolds did in the movie of the same name," she said one day and went out and rented the video. She brought it to my uncle's and we roared with laughter over the character's trials and tribulations, even though some of them hit very close to home. Today, for the first time, I'd seen Diane as weak and helpless. I didn't want to acknowledge I was disappointed in her but, by the time I finally drifted toward sleep, I was doing just that.

I don't know what woke me — voices perhaps or the barking of a dog -- but I heard something. The little clock on the dresser said five of four. I slid out of bed and without putting on a light stood by the open window. A breath of cool air ruffled the curtains. It was colder here than at the lake. I sensed movement on the grounds below and when I stepped closer to the window to look, I saw Diane hurrying across the lawn toward the drive. She motioned to someone hidden by a bank of shrubbery. This wasn't the same woman I'd said good night to a few hours before — the teary, clinging woman who'd thanked me over and over for staying with her. This Diane, dressed in a flowing white peignoir, her wild, tousled auburn hair straining against a white silk headband, looked like a woman racing to an illicit rendezvous. I watched as her visitor stepped forward into a shaft of light cast by one of the lamps along the drive. Tom Durocher.

I hadn't realized he was so much bigger than Diane when I saw them together at the inn. He towered above her, his head outlined against the sharp, leafless branch of a tree. Like a rack of horns, I thought, like pictures I'd seen of the Minotaur, huge and dark and menacing, pursuing one of the Greek maidens sent to Crete to dance merrily into his maze and be violated and devoured. Not getting enough sleep always gave me weird thoughts, but even when I shook my head, I couldn't dislodge the image or the strange sense of foreboding it brought with it.

His hands were on her waist, roughly it seemed to me, possessively, and as I watched he untied the belt of her robe and reached up to yank it down sharply from her shoulders. His big hands shoved the satin-bound edges apart as he pulled her to him. She was naked under the robe. Her skin gleamed white in the lamplight; the face she turned up to him was as expressionless as a statue's. In one quick movement, he lowered his dark head to her breast and pushed her backward into the shadows out of my line of sight.

SIX

At six o'clock, after only an hour more of fitful sleep, I opened my eyes and saw the white wall opposite Jonathan's bed streaked with blood. My heart was knocking itself out of my chest by the time I realized I was staring at a poster of a rock group, its blood-red background overlaid with images similar to the ones that had tormented me during the night. Fragments of my nightmares came rushing back — knives and strawberry marks and fire, fire everywhere. The clean, fresh-smelling sheets I'd snuggled into so comfortably the evening before were drenched with perspiration.

My head pounded. I needed a quick jolt of caffeine, then I'd leave a note and be on my way. When I first met Diane, I'd figured her for the well-organized type and I was right. The coffee maker was set to start. I had only to switch it on.

The second the coffee was ready, I filled the biggest cup I could find and carried it to a wing chair in the corner of the living room -- a chair with a back high enough to support my head. I didn't think I could hold it up very long myself. I sipped the coffee, willing it to force open my pinched blood vessels. Through the sliding glass doors across from me, I could see a small slate patio separated from the patios on either side of it by shoulder-high brick walls. A pleasant retreat ordinarily, I supposed, but this morning I was relieved to notice a charley bar holding the sliders firmly in place.

My headache began to loosen its grip but my great mood of twenty-four hours before had vanished without a trace. I didn't like knowing there was a murderer lurking about, someone who'd been willing to take a life for reasons unknown to me. I didn't like thinking about Edward Maranville lying dead with that knife sticking out of him and his face and hand burned black, but I couldn't make the thoughts of him go away.

As I sat there with my eyes half closed, I sensed movement outside the doors. A man, visible only as a dark shadow silhouetted against the brightness of the yard, crossed the little patio and peered through the glass. I bolted upright, sending coffee splashing down the front of my clothes.

Before I could collect myself, Diane, barefoot and wearing her white peignoir, rushed across the room and flipped up the bar. "There's this wonderful new concept, John," she said, revving up the sarcasm as she clicked the lock and shoved the slider open. "Guests ring a doorbell at the front of the house and I let them in through the front door."

"Don't start, Diane." The man stepped inside quickly, sliding the screen closed behind him. "I didn't want to ring the bell and wake you if you were still asleep. I figured you had a pretty rough night."

Her face changed at his show of sympathy. "Oh, John, you've heard about Edward then?"

"Jack Whittemore notified me. He'd found out I was co-owner at the lake."

"When did he call you?" she asked.

"Late, really late. I don't think I ever fell back to sleep. I still don't believe it."

"It was awful seeing him like that, John. Ellen was there. She'll tell you."

John turned to me. "Ellen?"

Diane didn't jump in with introductions, so he and I murmured our names to each other and shook hands. I could picture him as a CPA easy enough. He was balding, with inquisitive blue eyes that seemed to notice everything. His suit had cost plenty; his silk tie was elegant but conservative, designed to inspire confidence. I almost expected to see little accountants on it. He didn't look like a man with a scandalous, secret sex life. Well, of course, it wasn't secret any more and who could be sure what anyone else was up to anyway?

I turned my attention back to my coffee. For one, quick second I wondered how those sharp eyes were evaluating me, but I didn't much care. I felt sure my beige slacks and ivory pullover looked as if they'd been slept in even though I'd treated them to a hang-up in Jonathan's closet for a few hours. And my blunt-cut black hair, which would have fallen obediently into place after a shampoo, probably gave new meaning to the words, bad hair day. I knew I was a mess, but in the real world finding a murder victim can be hazardous to one's appearance, even if television and movie heroines go through that ordeal without looking any the worst for it. I eased my head onto the back of the chair. The air coming in the door touched my face like a soothing hand.

"You must have been shocked too, John. You and Edward have been friends a long time," Diane said.

He nodded. "I'd call Edward a client rather than a friend, but we do go back a lot of years. What about you? Are you okay now?"

"I guess." Diane walked over to the counter and poured herself a cup of coffee without offering him any. The white robe was tightly belted around her waist -- a modest variation on last night's look.

"They said you were pretty bent out of shape."

I watched for her reaction. He could have said blitzed or smashed or a number of other things and she couldn't have denied them. Still, I wondered why he'd said anything at all.

She didn't take the bait. "What did Jack tell you? Do they have any idea who did it?"

"Not yet, I guess. Edward's been rough on everyone the last few years. A lot of people have been turned off by him."

"Enough to kill him?"

"Diane, somebody did. He had some questionable deals going — just between you and me, of course. That's why I didn't want him to use the summerhouse."

"Yes, you were certainly adamant about that." The warmth that had been creeping into her voice disappeared. "Did you ever call him after you talked to me and tell him you didn't want him to stay there?"

He raised his right hand to his temple and frowned as if he were trying to remember. "No, I don't believe I ever touched base with him about it."

"That figures." The words conveyed her disgust with him.

"You know it might be a good idea if you didn't tell Whittemore I was ticked off."

"Ticked off? Ticked off is putting it mildly."

The lines across his forehead deepened. "Okay, so I was pretty sharp with you that night on the phone when I found out you'd told him he could use the place. I'm sorry -- if that's what you want to hear."

Diane banged her coffee cup down on the end table and opened the floodgates holding her anger in check. "Actually, John, I don't much care what I hear from you about anything. But let's not forget -- you're the one who started letting him use the summerhouse after we'd promised each other we wouldn't do that. I only said yes because I thought you'd already agreed to it and I didn't want another fight."

"I know, I know." He was obviously upset too but he kept his tone conciliatory, in marked contrast to hers. "Look, Edward's affairs are complicated. I'd like to keep Whittemore from poking around any more than necessary until I straighten a few things out. Would it be so damn hard for you not to tell him I was annoyed?"

"John, to tell you the truth, I'm not at all sure what I told Jack Whittemore last night. I really was — how did you put it so delicately? — bent out of shape. It was terrible finding Edward dead like that. Terrible. You can't imagine. I keep seeing him lying there, burned and stabbed and his hand, his poor hand."

"Don't," John said. "I don't want to hear about it. I can't stop thinking about it either. And I'm not totally insensitive, you know. I'm sure it's got to be worse for you."

Diane picked up her cup and took long, slow sips of her coffee. I sensed she was making an effort to calm herself. "The thing is I'm not sure what I said or didn't say. Maybe I did tell him I was the one who let Edward use our place and you'd gotten mad at me about it."

John slammed his hands down on the arms of his chair and bounced to his feet in one smooth move, not at all what you'd expect from a sedentary accountant. His face reddened. "Great. Make him think I did it. Thanks a lot, Diane."

I felt as if I were watching two kids on a seesaw. I expected him to punctuate his remark by storming out but he collected himself one more time. "Well, he's going to talk to you again today or tomorrow. Try not to get me thrown in jail if you can possibly help it."

Diane let the remark hang there. She got up slowly and stood near the front door, obviously waiting for him to leave. I could see her sending a student who'd misbehaved to the principal's office with exactly the same expression. Neither of them said good-bye. As soon as John went out, Diane closed the door firmly behind him.

"Ellen, I'm sorry you had to hear all that. You probably think we're terrible people. We didn't used to be, but I guess the divorce has brought out the worst in both of us. If you'll wait until I get dressed, I'll ride back to the lake with you and pick up my car."

I couldn't refuse. "All right, but I need to get going. This is a work day for me — at least it should be."

She refilled my cup and ran upstairs to dress. I heard John's tires squeal as he backed out of the parking lot.

SEVEN.

Diane dressed quickly -- I gave her credit for that -- but on the ride back to the lake she insisted on updating me with more details about her life with John.

Take their place on Lake George, for example. It meant a lot to her, I could see that. She always called it their summerhouse, never their camp, the name most lakeside residents here used even when the camps were luxurious second homes. She and John had bought the place from his father's sister shortly after they were married. The aunt had offered it to them at a good price but it was still far more than they could afford. John was just starting out as a CPA, but he recognized a good deal when he saw one and Diane had agreed. Even though they knew they'd be in over their heads financially, they went for it, managed to hang on until John's business was established. Still, buying it had meant a lot of sacrifices.

Like what sacrifices? I wanted to ask. I'm always curious when people open the door a crack and give you a peek into their private lives and then slam it shut.

Diane didn't explain.

Once they owned a place on the lake, they were shocked to find how many of their acquaintances-friends of theirs, clients of John's — asked to use it in the spring and fall when the Andersons weren't staying there themselves. Most of them gave lip service to the idea of paying rent, but whether they would have paid or not really wasn't the point. Diane and John thought of their summerhouse as their second home, not a rental property.

"I could never do that to friends, put them on a spot like that by asking to rent their summerhouse. Could you?" she asked me.

"Well," I murmured, thinking that was exactly what I'd done to my uncle, telephoned him out of the blue after things turned sour for me in New York and asked if I could stay at his camp. It had been empty for a long time so I hadn't seen the request as anything out of line. My aunt had died years before, and Ray had surprised everyone by moving farther north on the lake to become a volunteer at a bat sanctuary near Hague. My uncle realized late in life he liked bats better than people and, even though I didn't share his enthusiasm for the beady-eyed little creatures, some days I wondered if he wasn't onto something.

As for Diane and John, they'd solved their problem easily enough. They simply refused all would-be renters and borrowers — said they'd promised each other never to loan out the place to anyone. That worked fine, or seemed to. Then, last spring Diane had found out quite by accident that Edward Maranville was staying there, staying with John's approval. She'd been furious; they'd had a terrible argument about it, but John wouldn't back down. Edward was an important client. End of discussion.

That morning in the car Diane became more and more upset as she told me the story. "The worst part of it was, this wasn't the first time Edward had stayed there. John had let him use the place several times before and never told me," she said.

"But I thought Edward was a friend of yours, as well as a client of John's. Am I missing something here?"

"I wouldn't call Edward a friend exactly."

Almost the same words John had used. Didn't anyone want to acknowledge the man as a friend?

Diane hesitated, searching for a way to explain. "Edward and I belonged to a couple of the same art groups, went to parties at one another's houses occasionally. He has a lovely home in Glens Falls, by the way. Our summerhouse is nowhere near as elegant. I never quite understood why he wanted to stay there — he didn't enjoy the lake that much."

"So what are you saying, Diane? I still don't understand."

"I'm saying Edward was a bright man, entertaining, fun to talk with, especially about art, but he was a user. I know it's not right to speak ill of the dead, but Edward was always looking for ways to take advantage of people."

"And you felt he was taking advantage of John?"

"I'd have to say so."

"Was he a struggling artist?"

"No, not at all. He was an amateur painter but I don't think he ever expected to sell any of his work. He lived very well. Lived beyond his means, I suspect from remarks John let slip. He owned fabulous antiques and Oriental rugs. Didn't hold a job or anything tacky like that. Came from a wealthy European family who lost everything during World War II. Romanian, I think. Edward managed to save part of the family art collection, but the lands and money were long gone."

"And John handled his business affairs?"

"Edward started with John when he first moved to Glens Falls. That was about ten years ago"

"And this fall, when you told Edward he could stay

at the lake, John suddenly changed his mind and didn't want him there?" None of this made much sense to me. Was John just being perverse, I wondered.

"Well, I guess he'd changed his mind before this fall, but he hadn't bothered to let me know. Believe me, I would have been happy to say no. I didn't because I wanted to avoid another argument with John. We've had so many battles over the divorce, you wouldn't believe it."

"So John blew up at you, but wouldn't call Edward himself and tell him he couldn't use the place."

"That was typical of John. He can be a real wimp when it comes to his clients. He's got a reputation as a nice guy every place but home and he's not about to wreck it."

I'd heard more than enough about John Anderson for one day. What I really wanted was the skinny on Tom Durocher. I ran up a trial balloon. "I'm too tired to sort through all this right now. I didn't sleep very well last night, did you?"

"I know what you mean. I feel as if I hardly slept at all. But it meant a lot that you stayed with me. I really appreciated it, Ellen." She reached across and patted my arm in an affectionate gesture.

I didn't let the kind words deter me. "I heard voices about four o'clock. I got up and looked out. There was a man outside near the drive."

Diane bit down on her lip frowning, as if puzzling over how much to tell me. She went for a casual approach. "Oh, I know who you saw. Tom Durocher stopped by to see if I was all right. He's nice like that, but it was so late I didn't want to ask him in."

"Really? He stopped by at four o'clock in the morning? He must be quite a friend."

"He's a bartender, you know. Four o'clock in the morning means nothing to him."

EIGHT

The minute Diane left that morning, I pulled my old sweats out of the closet and laced on my running sneaks. I wasn't sure how far I could go on my bum knee but, if I expected to get any work done, I needed to clear my head. The dirt road that circled behind the camps on the horseshoe-shaped cove made a perfect place to run. The year-round residents on the ridge above kept to themselves; the summer people who owned the camps along the shore had left for the season. I had this particular corner of the world to myself.

I did a few stretching exercises, flexing my knee. I told myself it didn't hurt as much as it had the day before. I'd start at half speed, then step it up if I could. Most days I charged out of Ray's back door and headed toward the promontory on the right-hand side of the cove. I ran straight up to the rocks at the water's edge, circled back past Ray's camp and out the left side of the cove, then home. A perfect short course.

On the way I was immersed in some of the most magnificent fall color I'd ever seen, treated to breathtaking views of the lake and the islands and mountains to the north. Lake George might not have an elegant name, thanks to the British who'd changed it from Lac du Saint Sacrement when they routed the French, but the lake and its environs certainly ranked as one of the most beautiful places on earth.

On a day like this when the air was sparkling clear, I'd swear I could see Ticonderoga thirty-two miles away on the lake's northern tip. And with Ray's neighbors gone, the only sounds I'd hear would be the slap of water against docks and shore and the low rustle of wind in the trees. I'd be able to block all thoughts of Edward Maranville and all my concerns about Diane Anderson and the dorky men in her life right out of my head.

At least I thought I'd be able to. I managed to brainwash myself pretty well during my run but I hadn't expected my teenage friend, Josie Donohue, to be waiting at my kitchen door when I staggered across the imaginary finish line in my uncle's yard a little past noon.

Josie was Kate's daughter, although nothing about the girl would suggest the relationship. I'd met her several months before at her mother's restaurant when I was taking photographs for a feature article I was doing on Kate's catering business. As I was packing up my camera, Josie had sidled up to me and asked, "How do you get to be a writer?"

The underlying desperation I sensed in the girl struck a chord, transported me back to a time when I too was frantic to escape the misery of my sixteen-year-old world. Been there, done that, I thought. So I'd struck up a conversation with Josie and, before I knew it, I was agreeing to read some of her poetry, poetry which turned out to be surprisingly good. Our friendship had progressed from there.

At least it had progressed until now. Today she was hurt and anxious to make sure I knew it. She followed me inside, almost bowling me over when I stopped to pull the key out of the door and massage my aching knee. "Tell me it's not true. Tell me you didn't find a dead body and not call me. I don't f'ing believe it."

"Down, girl. The phone at Diane's was out of order and you know once the sheriff's department gets involved those guys have their own ideas on who gets called and who doesn't."

To my surprise, she bought my hasty improvisation. "I can't believe my rotten luck not being with you, but tell me everything and we'll start figuring out who did it. You said we were partners in crime, remember?"

"I may have used the expression partners in crime at some time, but I wasn't suggesting we could be partners in crime solving. And back up a minute. Aren't you supposed to be in school now?"

My remark elicited a snort and a semi-obscene gesture. I got the message. Josie at sixteen was so much like I'd been at that age it scared me. Her teenage angst, her determination to remain the outsider, her antipathy toward everything and everybody, especially toward Kate, who to me seemed the most level-headed of parents, scored even higher on the Richter scale than mine had in those long ago days. But, possibly because she sensed a kindred spirit in me as I did in her, she'd stamped me with her seal of approval and let me into her small circle of friends.

"I'm ditchin'. This is more important. Anyway, I don't have a class until one-thirty. So tell me," she said.

If I satisfied her curiosity, maybe I could send her off to school in time for her class and get to work myself without losing too much of the afternoon. As I fixed us each a tuna fish sandwich, I gave her a fast run-through of Sunday's events -- the fire, the dead man with the knife sticking out of him, the mysterious figure racing down the stairs, even my surprise at the brightly lighted room. When she insisted on a graphic description of Edward Maranville's charred face and hand, I suffered another attack of the queasies. Josie didn't bat an eye

Finally, after she'd asked as many questions about the crime scene as Jack Whittemore, she said, "So when you went to the Marlborough House, did you see Tom Terrific?"

"Who?"

"You know. Tom Terrific, the bartender. That's what we call him. Ms. Anderson's hottie."

"Her what?"

"Her hottie, her squeeze. You know what I mean."

I burst out laughing. Leave it to Josie. "Yes, I guess I do."

"Those two think it's a big secret but the kids all know they're gettin' it on, have been for a long time."

Now I was even more puzzled that Diane hadn't told me. "How long a time?"

"Jake saw 'em together over in Vermont at least two years ago. Very kissy face."

"Jake saw them?" Josie's own hottie might have a future in the detective business himself.

"That's what he told me. They never go out in public any place around here, I don't think."

Two years ago. Before Diane discovered her husband's infidelity with Sydney Vanderhoff. Interesting. But why would she and Tom keep their relationship secret now that Diane was divorced? "Is Tom married? Is that why they aren't seen together?"

"Never heard he was. I'll find out."

"Scratch that. Let's not stir anything up. There's something else you can do, if you will."

Spots of pink appeared on Josie's cheeks. For a moment she actually looked pretty. I couldn't help thinking as I had so many times before what a difference a touch of makeup and a decent haircut would make in this girl. When I first met her, she was a PIB, one of those people in black you find on high school and college campuses whose outlandish black garments proclaim their refusal to be part of the mainstream. I'd been pleased when Josie renounced that particular fashion statement, even took a little credit for the change. When she unveiled her new wardrobe of tattered jeans from the second-hand store, I thought she'd taken a step in the right direction -- but it was a very small step. The faded cutoffs she was wearing wouldn't rate as an improvement over anything.

"Really? You've got an assignment for me?" Josie leaned forward, flashing a Cheshire cat grin. As she slicked her dark hair back from her face, I noticed one of her ears had been pierced in several new places. A row of silver studs now outlined the entire curve of her right ear.

I bit down hard on my tongue and waited until the urge to comment had passed. "I guess you could think of it as an assignment. Tom told us Mr. Maranville and some of his friends were really interested in Georgia O'Keeffe. Got me thinking. I'd like to see the house she stayed in. Do you know where it's located?"

"It's gone now, I think, and she only stayed there summers usually. Our teacher told us her husband's family owned a house on the lake. What was his name? Stieglitz, that was it. He was some big shot photographer. Then, there was another place she stayed, up on a hill somewhere. I can find out.

"What kind of paintings did she do when she lived around here?"

"We studied her in art class last year. She's famous for those paintings of cows' skulls, but she painted other stuff when she lived at Lake George."

"Like...?"

Josie shrugged. "I forget. Buildings, the lake, stuff like that."

"Tom said these men asked a lot of questions."

"And you think this has something to do with the murder?" Her eyes widened.

"Nothing that dramatic. We talked about Georgia O'Keeffe because I'd gone up there Sunday intending to interview Mr. Maranville about her. I'm planning to write a feature article about her. Not a feature like the one I did on your mother's catering business. This one would have to be longer. I need to gather tons of information before I start writing. I thought maybe you'd help me."

"But El, that's not crime solving. I want us to crack this murder case."

"And get ourselves murdered too? Forget that." If I wanted to find out more about Edward Maranville's murder, I'd do it by myself. I wasn't going to put Josie at risk.

"Anyway, what about your career advice book? I thought you were all hot to finish that," she said

"I can take time off for something like this. It's a great topic and I need the money."

"Money, shmoney. El, you're backin' out on me."

"This isn't backing out. There's no money in amateur detecting but I'd pay you to help me research Georgia O'Keeffe. You could pick up a few extra bucks, buy more earrings or something."

Josie looked ready to throw the remains of her sandwich at me. "Right."

"Listen. I'm talking big time here. New York Times maybe. This could make us famous. I'll pay you by the hour or give you a percentage of my earnings, if you'd like that better."

"But you're not even sure anybody'll buy your article, are you?" The kind of remark an aspiring feature writer really needs.

"Hey. Pull that knife out of my back and have a little faith in me," I said.

"Okay, okay. But only because I like hangin' with you. You can pay me by the hour. I can't be waitin' around for any percentage. What do you want me to do?"

"Can you find out if any of Georgia O'Keeffe's paintings are in museums around here?"

Josie shook her head. "I don't think they are."

"Could you find out for sure?"

"Sure. I got connects. I'll ask around."

"And find out if any are privately owned. Maybe your art teacher knows. See if she can give us names of people we could talk to, especially people who might remember O'Keeffe or the Stieglitz family."

"Wouldn't they be way old, El?"

"All the more reason to find 'em fast."

"Beam me up, Scottie. I already know one person -- Mrs. Cascadden. Her husband wrote a book about Georgia O'Keeffe. He's croaked, but she helped him with it. Ms. Benoit was always yakking in art class about how lucky we were to have people like them around here."

"Great. Maybe we can start with her, but let's get some other names too. I expect this project to be big."

Josie rolled her eyes, letting me know how appalled she was at my stupidity. "Big? Finding a murderer is big. Writing an article is kid stuff."

"Hey, kid stuff can turn into something big." I was referring to my New York Times aspirations, nothing more. I swear it.

Josie jumped to her feet. I'd hoped I was buying myself a few days of peace, but she looked alarmingly eager to get started

NINE

With Josie gone, I settled down to work. At least I tried to. Talking about the murder had reopened the Pandora's box of horrors and no matter how hard I tried I couldn't shove those horrors back into their box and forget them. When I did manage to think about something else for a few minutes, the pain in my knee catapulted me right back to Sunday afternoon.

Running had been a mistake. Even when I sat perfectly still, my knee burned like fire and that made me wonder about Edward Maranville and whether he was still alive when the fire was set and who could have done such an awful thing to him.

I watched the time, knowing Kevin would stop by as soon as he could. He'd called early in the afternoon, but as always when he telephoned from work, his remarks were guarded. Rating a private office at the Lake Protection Group, he'd told me on several occasions, didn't guarantee him privacy. Lake George Village was a small town and he and I had agreed the fewer people who knew of our relationship the better. Kevin had a fragile ex-wife and two young sons to consider and I wasn't looking for a designation of big city slut if I could avoid it.

Twice I thought Uncle Ray's old-fashioned schoolhouse clock had stopped but eventually the hands crept around to five o'clock. Kevin arrived at five-fifteen, seizing me in an unexpected bear hug the minute I opened the back door.

"I didn't want to say much on the phone," he said. "The women in the office are gaga over the murder anyway and the fact you and Diane Anderson were first on the scene has them crazed with curiosity. Are you sure you're all right?"

I nodded. "Beer or tea? I've OD'd on coffee in the last twenty-four hours. I can't face another cup."

"Tea then. I'd like to get all the details straight. I want you to go back to the beginning and tell me everything that happened. Tom drove me crazy with his interruptions yesterday."

I made tea and launched into my play-by-play account of Sunday's events. By this time I had it down pat. Kevin heard me out, stopping me periodically as he tried to fit the pieces of the puzzle together. The fire, we both thought, didn't seem like the work of a professional arsonist.

"Jack Whittemore said no accelerant was used. I guess that's the official terminology," I said.

"So that means someone didn't go there planning to burn the place down."

"I guess not, or he would have brought along whatever he needed. Apparently, the fire was an afterthought. And there were no signs of a break-in."

Our best-guess scenario went like this: Someone had come to see Edward, quarreled with him, then stabbed him with a long, thin knife -- a kind of fancy letter opener. Edward had been stabbed only once -- from what I'd seen -- but somehow the knife had hit a vital spot. The wound had proved fatal.

"So the murderer may have been somebody he knew," Kevin said.

"Or someone he let into the cottage anyway," I said.

We continued our speculations. The killer must have cast around for a way to cover up the crime, we decided. Then, too panicked to remove the knife, he'd pulled the bedding out of the closet, piled it on top of the body and set the fire, hoping the body would be destroyed along with the cottage and everything in it. Only the fire hadn't caught well. It had smoldered, charring the blankets and Edward's face and hand, but not flaring up enough to spread through the rest of the room.

Thinking about the fire still had the power to rattle me. "Break time. Let's talk about something else for a few minutes," I said.

I took some stew I'd picked up at Kate's restaurant from the refrigerator and started it heating on the stove. Not only had Kate become a good friend, her delicious take-out was solving most of my cooking problems. The stew, full of bright fall vegetables and glistening chunks of chicken, filled the kitchen with a fabulous aroma. When it was hot, I ladled it out into two of my aunt Mattie's earthenware bowls and stuck a plate of thick-sliced peasant boule on the worn pine table between us. The meal looked like something Martha Stewart would have been proud to serve.

While we ate, we continued our hiatus on murder talk out of respect for Kate's belief that food should be enjoyed in a pleasant, relaxed atmosphere.

"That Kate. You should have married her. How come you never thought of it?" I asked Kevin.

"Who says I never thought of it?" he said with a sly grin.

"Oh, oh. Are there things I haven't heard about you two?"

"Just kidding. Kate and I have been friends since

grade school, but I could never be married to her."

"Because of Josie?" I often wondered how long any man would put up with that girl's shenanigans. I'd witnessed more than one argument between her and Kevin.

"No, because I'd weigh three hundred pounds," he said. A neat sidestep.

When we'd both mopped up our last bites of stew, Kevin jumped to his feet and took his bowl to the sink. "Okay, crime time again. I've got to hear more about this."

I made more tea while Kevin built a fire in the fireplace. I refused to let the fire remind me of Edward. I concentrated on remembering Billy, the poor inept kid at the inn who needed his job but didn't seem to be very good at it.

"So where were we?" Kevin asked as we sat on the couch with our mugs, watching the flames take hold. "The phone was dead..."

As we drank our tea, I told him the part of the story he hadn't heard -- how someone who'd been hiding upstairs had rushed down the steps and shoved me.

The color drained from his face; even his lips went white. "What? The murderer was there all along?"

"I guess. I mean I guess it was the murderer. Somebody must have been upstairs all the time we were in the living room."

"You didn't see who it was?"

"No. It happened so fast. I went flying, almost hit the fireplace. I did an awful job on my knee."

"I thought you were limping more. Why didn't you tell me right away? This isn't general knowledge, I don't think. Is Jack keeping it quiet?"

"Maybe. I sort of hope he is. I really didn't see anyone but the murderer may think I did."

"Hadn't you planned to tell me?" The eyes behind the wire-rimmed glasses narrowed.

He was hurt, angry even. That I could see. "Of

course, Silly. You like to take everything in order. I was waiting 'til we got to the point when it happened."

He put his hands on my upper arms. I felt his fingers dig in hard through my sweater. "You're sure you planned to tell me? I don't like secrets between us."

"Of course I planned to tell you, Bluto."

He dropped his hands, tried for a lighter note. "Sorry, but you know I hate seeing you involved in things like this. And I don't want secrets between us, especially when somebody tries to kill you. Understood?"

"I don't think the person tried to kill me. I think he just wanted to get out of there without being seen."

"That's easy to say, Ellen. I don't like the way these things seem to happen to you."

"I know. You've made that quite clear. And I don't like being lectured about it," I said.

"Sorry again. Lecture over. So you didn't see the person who pushed you? Not even a quick glimpse?"

"No. I'm not even positive it was a man."

We both calmed down enough to speculate on whether the person who shoved me was Edward Maranville's murderer or someone else who'd been in the cottage when we got there and wanted to stay hidden.

"Either way, why would anyone hide upstairs if the cottage was on fire?" I asked Kevin. The same question I'd asked Jack Whittemore.

Kevin didn't have an answer either. "You're right. That doesn't make any sense."

We were so caught up in our talk I didn't think to mention the smell I'd noticed. It seemed pointless anyway. If I'd caught sight of the guy, maybe that would help identify him, but a smell? No way that would help, especially when I didn't even know what the smell was.

Finally, it was my turn to ask the questions. "What's the story on Diane and Tom Durocher? Josie says everyone knows they see each other, but Diane's never let on to me."

Kevin showed no surprise. "That's what you call a badly kept secret. I suppose she's afraid of flak from the school board, but I can't imagine why anyone would care. He's younger than she is and she was his teacher once a long time ago. Big deal."

"A shame, isn't it? After her bad times with John, it would be nice if she could enjoy life for a while," I said.

Kevin hesitated for a few seconds, then spoke slowly as if choosing his words with care. "I'm not sure how much you know about Diane's divorce, but not everybody blamed John. Diane can be difficult. She turns some people off." He pulled back as if he expected me to attack him in a display of feminist support.

"Kate has nothing but good things to say about her," I said, forgetting for the moment I'd been a little turned off by Diane myself the day before. "Are you telling me you guys are in John's corner on this one? Why am I not surprised?"

"Kate likes everyone. You and I might have some gender differences here. You're aware they exist, right?"

"Unfortunately, yes." I drew myself up, ready to launch into a defense of Diane Anderson worthy of a Scott Turow attorney.

Kevin took my teacup out of my hand and reached across me to set it on the end table. He put his hands on both sides of my face and kissed me with a long, thoroughly intoxicating kiss that sent me spinning light years away from Diane and John Anderson and their problems.

"You consider gender differences unfortunate?" he murmured, hovering over me.

I tried to stare him down. He had a great face, not just handsome but intelligent and kind. No one could ask more of a face than that. "Well, perhaps gender differences aren't always unfortunate," I conceded.

He took hold of the bows of his glasses and lifted them off. He leaned across me again to set the glasses on the table. I caught a faint hint of his morning after shave and felt his body, trim and muscular, pressed against mine. The removal of the glasses always signaled that something very pleasurable was about to happen. It did, and my defense of Diane Anderson had to be postponed to another day.

TEN

At nine o'clock the next morning, I took the last empty stool at the counter of Kate Donohue's little restaurant and plunged into a hotbed of talk. Herb the Baker, counterman and gossip lover extraordinare, presided over a full house, his drooping cheeks crisscrossed by smile lines, his usual hangdog look replaced by one of feverish animation. Most of his patrons at this hour were uniformed working men-- truckers, delivery men, power company employees -- with a few retirees sprinkled through the crowd. Everyone at both the counter and the four small tables had joined in a conversation about -- what else? -- the murder.

I ordered coffee and let the talk swirl around me.

"The quare fella, the one who hung around the inn?" a grizzled Adirondacker asked, throwing out the question to anyone who would answer.

"That's the one, Pete," a trucker said. "He owned a house in Glens Falls, they tell me, but he spent a lot of time at the inn. Don't ask me why."

"I can tell you why," a man with a Budweiser insignia on his shirt answered. "I sell beer up there. He was friends with some guys stayed there at lot."

"Friends?" the truck driver asked with a sneer.

"Hell, who knows? He wasn' t hurtin' anybody, far as I know."

"Musta hurt somebody enough to get hisself killed," Pete said.

"They don't know why he got killed, Pete. Maybe he surprised some vagrant breaking in to find a place to sleep."

"Heard he was hacked to pieces," Pete said.

"Stabbed once, we told you."

"Once? Can't kill nobody stabbing 'em once, can you?"

"Apparently this time you could. But never mind, I gotta go." The trucker pushed his chair back hard, scraping it along the floor. He shook his head as he made for the exit.

Before I could clear my own head, Kate held open the swinging door that led to her work area and motioned me inside. "I thought I saw you come in. What are you doing out this early?"

"Picking up the latest news on the murder."

"Just don't expect my customers to be one hundred percent accurate. You won't get the front page Times account here." She pulled up a stool to her work table for me.

"I suspected as much. Was Edward Maranville gay?"

"Probably, but low-key about it. No significant other, as far as anybody knew. If you're thinking some kind of lover's quarrel, I doubt it." Kate disappeared into her walk-in cooler and emerged carrying a tray of food. She set the tray down on the butcher block counter and began spooning seafood salad from a plastic container into a crystal bowl.

"Looks like you've got something special planned," I said.

"Luncheon. New client. Could be really good for

us." Kate decorated the top of her salad with a flower arrangement made from succulent-looking pink shrimp and strips of red and green pepper. As she lowered a piece of plastic wrap over the bowl, she paused, staring past me toward the back door. Diane Anderson, her jeans and bulky knit sweater indicating she'd taken another day off from school, had just come in.

"Kate," Diane said, her voice high-pitched and strained, "Kate, I really hate to ask you but I need a favor."

Kate pulled up a second stool. "Sit down. Tell me."

Diane patted my arm as she sat down. "I've got to go back to the summerhouse today. That's why I took the day off. John put pressure on the sheriff's department to hurry their investigation so he could get a cleaning service in and Jack Whittemore went along with it. Now I'd like to check the place out before the cleaners go in."

"Why the big rush? You're not going to be using it all winter, are you?" Kate asked

"John wants to turn off the water before it gets any colder. He's paying for the cleaning so I have to go along with him. He went through the house and says nothing's missing, but I want to see for myself."

"Hang on. Do they think the murderer went there to rob the place?" I said. That might explain what the man was doing upstairs. Maybe Kevin and I weren't so smart after all.

"They don't know anything yet. They haven't even released Edward's body to the funeral home. Ellen, I know you wouldn't want to go back there, but I thought maybe Kate would ride up with me. I can't face it alone."

"Not today, Diane. I'm doing a luncheon and I have no idea when I'll be through." Kate glanced in my direction, bouncing the question over to me.

I wouldn't have wanted to go back to that place alone either. I didn't make Diane ask me. I volunteered.

This time on the drive north along the lake, I prepared myself for the worst — although I didn't know what could be worse than what we'd seen on Sunday. As we approached the Anderson cottage, I was hit by an uncomfortable sense of déjà vu, but the sun was shining and the sky was a rich late-October blue and I assured myself there couldn't be anything more to fear in these tranquil surroundings.

I think we both shook a little as we walked up the porch steps. To my surprise, Diane reached into an empty flower pot and dug a key out of the dirt. She unlocked the front door and stared into the hallway before going in. I heard her quick intake of breath when she saw the living room. Spanish moss seemed to have sprouted from the ceiling; it took me a minute to realize I was seeing festoons of smoke hanging above us like giant gray cobwebs. If they'd been there Sunday, I hadn't noticed them. The furniture, shoved around at odd angles, probably by the rescue squad, was covered with a fine, gray silt. Diane's green and white print couch had taken on the color of a dirty lead pipe.

Diane took everything in without reacting. I thought she might cry out or wail or even curse the person who'd started the fire, but she stood there quietly, not saying a word. Then, she walked slowly into the kitchen.

The kitchen and the downstairs bedrooms and bath looked normal enough. Diane didn't comment, just nodded as she looked carefully around. Finally she said, "I guess I should be thankful only one room's affected."

I relaxed a little, but when we headed upstairs, it was my turn for a bad moment. The last time I'd stood in this hallway someone had been crouching on the staircase above me. Once again, I heard the strange whooshing noise he made as he rushed down the stairs, felt the blow to my head, the big hands shoving against my back, experienced the panic I felt as I hurtled forward, staggering across the living room. I recalled the odd unidentifiable odor I'd smelled that day and I shivered as I realized that I'd been as vulnerable to the killer's knife as Edward Maranville had been.

I followed Diane quickly up the narrow, enclosed staircase. The second story of the Anderson cottage was a smaller version of my uncle's place with a long corridor running from front to back and one large bedroom across the front similar to my bedroom at Ray's. The corridor was little more than a wide hallway with the roof sloping down almost to the floor on both sides and small cupboards built into the space beneath the eaves. On one side, someone had made a sitting area with a rocker and an occasional table and lamp, but the spot seemed much too dark for reading. A large closet with sliding doors had been built into a corresponding niche on the opposite wall.

"What's in there?" I asked.

"Storage. Old stuff from John's aunt that came with the house." Diane moved past the doors without stopping.

"Shouldn't we check it?" I asked

Diane nodded. "The closet's locked, but I'll get the key. There's a story connected with this stuff. There always is a story with John. When we bought this place from his aunt, his cousin Marie threw a fit. She lives in New Mexico -- has for years. She didn't want the place herself, but she thought we got too good a deal, I guess, because she made a terrific fuss about Aunt Gwendolyn's art work. That's how she always referred to it -- art work. Well, the art work consisted of a dozen or so paintings, all amateurish views of the lake."

"You mean the paintings came with the cottage?" I asked.

"Exactly. I didn't want to hang them and John didn't want to get rid of them, so he built this closet for them. Like Marie's going to turn up some day for her share. It's so ridiculous. But as long as we're here, we'll have to take a look."

I nodded. I didn't want to come back another time because we didn't check carefully enough.

Diane slipped into the bedroom and I heard the clatter of a drawer being pulled open. She came back with a small gold key and unlocked the sliding doors. Funny, I thought, if the paintings were worthless, why bother to keep them locked up?

Diane read my thoughts. As she pushed back one of the doors she said, "Silly, isn't it? More of John's wimpiness. He says Marie's made such a fuss, he never wants her to be able to say the paintings weren't stored properly."

The door slid open easily enough but the interior of the closet was black as a crypt.

"Hold on a minute." I dug into my shoulder bag for the flashlight on my key ring and shone the beam into the closet. A large painting, draped in a piece of sheeting, stood propped against the sloping back wall. A few pieces of bubble wrap lay on the floor near it. Otherwise the closet was empty.

Diane gave a little cry of surprise as she stepped through the doorway. "Something's wrong here. Flash that light around. There were at least a dozen paintings and now there's only one."

"Really? A dozen?"

"At least twelve, maybe fourteen. Not all the same size, but most of them as large or larger than this one. They were here a few months ago. We had trouble with bees. I remember seeing them when I sprayed."

"Mind if I take a closer look?" I asked.

When Diane nodded, I took hold of the painting with both hands and carried it into the bedroom. I set it on the floor by a window and lifted the sheet. It was a watercolor, more than two by three feet in size, a typical Lake George scene -- a part of the lake called the Narrows, complete with blue water and sky and a contingent of evergreens marching in stiff military formations up the bordering hills. The execution was as poor as Diane had said. A paint-by-number would have been more aesthetically pleasing.

"I hope Aunt Gwendolyn kept her day job," I said.

Diane stood next to me, staring at the painting and shaking her head. "Can you imagine hanging this in your living room?"

"Not unless I was the proud parent of a second grader and this was her work.".

"John would have hung them all, I think."

"You mean he liked the paintings, thought they were good?" My ex-fiance and I had disagreed more than once over art for our apartment. I was familiar with this territory.

"No. I don't think John thought they were any good," Diane said. "He just didn't want to take a stand with Marie. Said we should save the paintings so she could see for herself how worthless they really are -- if she ever decided to come here, that is."

"Who else has seen them?"

"Oh, I had them appraised. The expert agreed totally with my assessment, no value unless I wanted to think of them as cherished family heirlooms."

"And you didn't?"

Diane gave a disparaging wave. "Would you admit your family cherished this as an heirloom?"

"Could the frames be worth anything? Were they all like this one?" I stepped closer and ran my hand along the edge of the plain wooden frame. The finish had been dulled very little by time; the frame was richly grained with no gold or silver trim or inlays. Just the kind of simplicity I liked, but nothing out of the ordinary.

As Diane carried the painting back to the closet, I flashed the light around one more time. Neat rows of horizontal tracks, forming what looked like a double music staff in the dust, attested to the fact other paintings had been stored there.

Diane pointed to the tracks. "Look. You can tell the other paintings were in the closet until very recently. Now they're gone."

"Do you think John decided to send them to his cousin and didn't tell you?" I asked.

"With John anything is possible. But he would never have sent them all to her. You can bet your life on that. Still no one else could have taken them. Unless..."

The same thought struck us both at the same time. "The killer?" we said together.

Diane dismissed the idea immediately. "I don't think so. You see what the paintings looked like. Nobody would have killed for them. No, John must have done something with them. Maybe he just didn't bother to tell me."

I couldn't argue with her, but it was hard to believe this was only a coincidence -- their house guest murdered and paintings from a locked closet mysteriously disappeared.

ELEVEN

Late fall was a slow season at the Marlborough House Inn. By the time we arrived there at one-thirty, lunch was over and the dining room was empty. Diane steered me toward the rathskeller where Tom Durocher was setting up the bar for the cocktail hour.

I wasn't looking forward to seeing Tom again. The overly possessive way he'd treated Diane that night in her driveway still bothered me, but he greeted us warmly, as boyish and gentlemanly as an Eagle Scout.

Despite my lingering concerns, I agreed with Josie's assessment of him as a hottie. His face was slightly flushed -- I suspected Diane's arrival was responsible for that -- and the rolled up sleeves of his dress shirt gleamed dazzling white against arms still bronzed with summer tan. He set glasses of wine in front of us, saying "Compliments of the house."

"Thanks, but let's make this the only one," I said quickly, recalling the after-effects of the last complimentary drinks he'd served up. "We're here for a late lunch and then I have to get home."

"Lunch it is," Tom said as he handed us menus. Without asking where we wanted to eat, he set place mats and silverware in front of us on the bar. Smooth.

We ordered turkey clubs and Tom relayed the order by phone to the kitchen.

"Do they have any ideas yet about who killed Edward?" he asked. He pulled a dish of orange slices and maraschino cherries from under the bar and began threading the fruit onto green plastic skewers shaped like little swords.

"I haven't heard a thing. I know Edward rubbed people the wrong way sometimes, but I can't imagine who'd want to kill him, can you?" Diane said.

"Didn't you tell me he was always bucking up against the old guard in those arts organizations he was in?"

"Hazel Dunklee, Jim Patterson, people like that. Not exactly the type who do murder," Diane said.

"What were those friends of his like, the ones who stayed here?" I asked.

"You saw one the other night, remember? He came in for a drink while you two were waiting for Jack. Big guy, light hair, Bertholdt Ulrich's his name. He was really shook. Heard there'd been a murder and had just found out it was Edward. Couldn't even talk about it. Downed his Scotch and left."

"The man who sat at the end of the bar?" I said.

"That's the one. The other friend had already gone back to New York. Bertholdt had to call him and he was dreading it." Tom studied his completed garnishes and arranged them one by one in a silver bowl. They looked good enough to turn me on to cocktails -- like I needed more bad habits.

"How did they get along with Edward?" I said.

"Oh, the three of them argued all the time, especially Edward after he'd had a few drinks. One time he carried on so much one of 'em called him a raging queen. But that's the way they were -- made really mean cracks to each other but that was the end of it. Edward was such a talker. He drove people nuts sometimes."

"And you were setting me up with him, Diane? Thanks a lot," I said.

"For an interview, remember. Edward was a compulsive talker, but that would have been perfect for your purposes. You could have asked him one question and he'd have run his mouth all afternoon," she said.

Tom gave her a reproving look. "Diane, that's not like you. Edward did get all cranked up, especially about art, but he was a smart guy."

"I know, I know. I'm just upset by all this. Sorry." She slid her glass forward and Tom refilled it quickly.

I put my hand over mine and shook my head. I'd have to stay alert if I didn't want a repeat of Sunday night.

"So has Jack Whittemore been here asking questions?" Diane asked.

"I'm just the bartender, remember. I heard he came and asked Trev some questions but nobody's talked to me."

"Trev's the owner here, Jim Trevellyan," Diane said.

Tom's face flushed a darker red. "Correction: the owner's son."

She'd touched a nerve. I could see that.

Diane recapped the family history. "The Marlborough House is one of the mansions built along this side of the lake in the last century. Old Mr. Trevellyan inherited it from his parents, raised his family here. A few years ago young Trev and his wife talked him into turning the place into an inn. Rumor is Trev wants to take over the business but the father isn't ready to trust him with it yet."

"Jack talked to both Trev and the old man. If he'd bothered to ask me, I might have told him to talk to the friends too, but I'm only the bartender. What would I know?" Tom said.

A little too much self-pity for my taste. I interrupted. "Jack's a smart guy. Don't you think he's found out they were friendly with Edward and talked to them? What's happened to our lunches anyway?"

I'd barely gotten the words out when Billy Harris brought our sandwiches from the kitchen. He looked as ill at ease as he had the first time I saw him. He dropped the plates with a clatter at the end of the bar and, after a quick peek in our direction, scuttled away.

"Teenagers, so self-conscious about everything," Diane said, smiling after him.

Tom went for the plates and arranged them on our mats with a flourish.

I took a big bite of my sandwich. Delicious. "Tom, while we eat tell us more about Edward's friends," I said.

"Bertholdt stays here the most. In his late forties, I'd say, slight accent, Eastern European, I guess. Not too friendly to me after I made the mistake of calling him Bert one night. But he was always buttering up Trev or the old man, angling for a special deal on his rooms."

"Rooms?" I asked.

"They like a suite. Nothing so common as a room. The other one, Charles Renault, is younger and nicer, but he isn't here as often. Easygoing guy, peacemaker type, at least when he's sober. I thought sometimes they stirred him into the mix as a buffer."

"Do you think they're involved in the murder?"

"No signs they were, but I wouldn't put it past Bertholdt to rub somebody out."

Maybe it was just as well Jack Whittemore hadn't talked to Tom. Unfounded accusations didn't set well with Jack.

Diane and I went on eating our sandwiches. I crunched a sweet potato French fry. Even the inn's fries were superb.

"You said the men asked questions about Georgia

O'Keeffe? I asked Tom.

"Yeah, wanted to know exactly where the Stieglitz family home was located."

"It was near here, right?" I said.

"Just up the lake. A big house on the water called Oaklawn."

Diane murmured her approval. Once again, I pictured her in her classroom, this time dishing out positive reinforcement.

"I'm impressed. How come you know so much about Georgia O'Keeffe?" I said.

"Trev insists people who work here be able to answer the guests' questions about the area. Thinks it's good for business. One of his few pronouncements I agree with."

"So Edward's friends were really interested in her?" I said.

"Couldn't get enough of her. Wondered if anyone up here owned any of her paintings, stuff like that. They were always whispering like they knew something nobody else did."

"Diane," I started to say, "you don't suppose..."

I felt a sharp kick on my shin, fortunately not on my bad leg. I dropped the subject fast.

"Are there people around here who remember her?" I asked, but I was only half listening. I was thinking about Diane's missing paintings. If they all looked like the one I saw, they couldn't possibly have been done by Georgia O'Keeffe, but still...

"A few of the older folks remember her," Tom was saying, "and others can tell you what their parents said about her. In fact, one of Bertholdt's biggest fights with Charlie started over that very thing. Charlie had gone into Bolton and asked if anyone remembered Georgia O'Keeffe. Bertholdt got furious with him."

"What's so terrible about that?" I asked.

"I didn't know either. The three of them were sitting at that little table over there by the window. All hell broke loose. Bertholdt told Charlie to shut up, lay off that kind of talk. He was drunk, I guess, but the funny thing was Edward seemed to agree with him. Usually it was the out-of-towners ganged up on poor old Ed."

Diane shoved her plate away. "Oh, let's stop talking about the murder. I can't get that body out of my mind anyway and the more we talk about it, the worse I feel."

Fine with me. I didn't want to think about the murder either. I was much more interested in those missing paintings. If somehow, some way, paintings by Georgia O'Keeffe actually turned up in Lake George, the timing couldn't be better. I'd have a perfect peg for my feature.

My luck was changing for the better. My O'Keeffe article wouldn't be fodder for the Post Standard. I could see it featured on a double page spread in the New York Times. I pictured my ex-fiancé Tim stumbling on it as he ate his Sunday croissants, heard my former boss Roger and the others at the agency gasping with surprise, imagined my New York friends phoning each other with the news. "That Ellen. Isn't she something? Things go wrong for her and she comes right back swinging."

Optimism was my state of choice that day. I had no idea how much Diane Anderson was going to mess up my life.

TWELVE

The next forty-eight hours went by in a whirl. I searched for Georgia O'Keeffe on the Internet and found a number of sites. I made a run to Crandall Library in Glens Falls and signed out or photocopied everything I could find on O'Keeffe and her work, scavenging both from the stacks and from the library's special local history collection. Fascinating stuff.

O'Keeffe had already spent one summer on her own at Lake George before she came to the Stieglitz family home for the first time in 1918. From her earliest years in Wisconsin, she'd been sensitive to the land and to the wonders of nature and she found inspiration in the upstate New York setting -- in its trees, leaves, flowers, barns, even in the hills surrounding the lake. As her paintings became more abstract, she chose the skies above the lake and the clouds and wild electrical storms as subjects, often representing the same images in her paintings that Stieglitz captured in his photographs.

I was immersed in comparing some of these Equivalents, as O'Keeffe called them, when I looked up to see Josie Donohue waving frantically through the kitchen window.

She glared at me when I opened the door as if I'd committed the crime of the century. "I practically knocked the skin off my knuckles and you didn't even hear me," she complained as she pushed past me. "The wind almost tore your present to pieces. Diane ordered you one of my masterpieces."

Josie set the large basket she was carrying on the kitchen table. Wrapped in clear cellophane and trimmed with a cascade of orange ribbon, the basket held a pyramid of gleaming fruit, so perfect it looked artificial, ringed by little sacks of fancy crackers and cookies.

"Did you arrange this? It's beautiful," I said, genuinely impressed.

"Yeah, I did it. Diane always has me do the baskets she sends people. Says I do an A+ job with them."

"I'd go along with that if they all look like this. But why is she sending me a present?"

Josie fished a letter out of the pocket of her jean jacket. "Here. She wrote you this to explain."

In her note Diane apologized again for dragging me into what she called "her messy life" and thanked me for my support. She pushed all the right buttons -- came across as warm, sincere, totally believable. I was touched by the gift and the note but what pleased me most was Josie's pride in her creation. With her gift Diane had not only patronized her friend's business, she'd given her friend's daughter a badly needed boost in self-esteem. For that she deserved an A+ herself.

I found a Pepsi in the refrigerator for Josie and undid the ribbon holding the cellophane on the basket handle. "Let's see if this stuff tastes as good as it looks. Which one of these treats will we open first?"

"The cheese sticks are to die for. They get my vote."

I lifted the pack out carefully and opened it. Josie was right. The cheese sticks were melt-in-your-mouth delicious.

Josie prowled around the camp taking everything in. "You found all these books on Georgia O'Keeffe? Are you sure she doesn't have something to do with the murder?" she asked.

"Only if she arranged it from beyond the grave." I hummed a few bars of Twilight Zone music.

"Don't weird out on me, El. I asked my art teacher like I said I would. She told me to come in tomorrow after school and she'd give me the names of some people you could talk to."

"Good going," I said. Then, for the rest of the package of cheese sticks and an apple so fabulous looking it would have tempted Adam all over again, we sealed our deal. Josie would be my research assistant. I'd pay her for her help and all crime solving activities would remain in Jack Whittemore's large and capable hands -- at least as far as Josie knew. If I wanted to find out more about the murder and Diane's missing paintings, I'd do it on my own.

When I heard the tap on my back door a few hours later, I didn't think it could be Kevin. He'd been out of town at a conference for several days and I didn't expect him back until the weekend. But my heart did a little thump of anticipation. Maybe he was rushing back, as anxious to see me as I was to see him.

I'd been reading on the couch with my leg tucked under me and I almost went sprawling when I took my first step. My foot had gone numb except for the million needles sticking into it. I hobbled to the door and flung it open. I couldn't hide my disappointment when I found Diane Anderson standing there. She was holding the watercolor we'd seen at her summer house.

"You probably can't believe I'd ask another favor of you." She banged the painting down on the kitchen floor and dropped into a chair at the table. She looked agitated again, her hair tossed around by the wind and her eyes dark with a haunted look that made me wonder if she was on the verge of another meltdown.

"Now what's wrong?" I said.

She winced at my words. "I don't blame you for being disgusted with me, but I couldn't stop thinking about the paintings. You're the only one who knows they're missing. That's why I didn't want you to say anything in front of Tom. I think John's done something with them and I want to leave this one here with you until I can find out."

She was right: I was disgusted. The good vibes I'd felt for her only a few hours earlier faded fast. "Diane, take the stupid thing home to your condo. John won't even know you have it. Then call Jack Whittemore and report the others missing."

"I can't. I've got to talk to John first. If I take this home, he'll find it. I know he gets in when I'm not home."

"Change the locks," I said.

She looked even more hurt. "Oh, Ellen, you must think I'm an awful dope. I have changed the locks. I think John takes Jonathan's key on their weekends together and copies it. I have the feeling John can let himself in any time he wants to."

"You don't actually think he'd sneak in and take this, do you?"

"He took the others, didn't he? There's something about this painting, something we don't know. Maybe Georgia O'Keeffe really did paint it."

Seeing the watercolor again dispelled whatever faint suspicions I'd been harboring. "Georgia O'Keeffe? Not on her worst day. All you have to do is look at it. And you said the others were very similar to this one."

"Please let me leave it here, Ellen. Do anything you want with it. Toss it in the lake for all I care." Her eyes filled with tears; she wiped her hand across them, smearing eye shadow and liner down her cheeks.

"I'm going to make you coffee and feed you some of

those scrumptious treats you sent me. Then maybe you'll stop driving yourself nuts over an ugly painting that's been sitting in a closet for years. Diane, you've got to get a grip."

"I can't take it home with me, Ellen. I can't let John get this painting away from me the way he's gotten everything else. I'll think of some place else to store it. Just give me a couple days. Please."

Her nose was dripping and she didn't even notice. Diane Anderson -- attractive, well-groomed Diane Anderson -- was standing in front of me with her eye makeup smudged, her face a mass of red blotches and her nose running like crazy and she was too upset to realize, much less care. So what could I do? I agreed to keep the painting.

Diane calmed down a little after a cup of decaf and a cookie but she was still seething when she left. Why was she so upset, I wondered. Yes, she was angry at John, but was there something else going on here? They'd battled like tigers over the divorce, I knew, with Diane inevitably coming out the loser. Did she have some hidden agenda I knew nothing about? Or was it that she really couldn't handle another loss, even an insignificant one?

I paced around the camp until I almost wore a path in the carpet, then threw Aunt Mattie's granny square afghan over my shoulders and went out to stand on the front porch. Most of the year-round homes on the east side had gone dark. It was freezing cold. Off to my left the lights of Lake George Village spread wavy, elongated reflections onto the dark waters of the lake. If I leaned out over the porch rail, I could see the huge bulk of the Lac du Saint Sacrement, the largest of the lake steamers, as it tossed restlessly at its dock.

I shivered and pulled the afghan more tightly around me. The wind howled down the lake with the fury of a Huron war party. I could almost hear the screams of the captives tomahawked and scalped after the British surrendered Fort William Henry to the French and Montcalm lost control of his Indian allies. This end of the lake had been marked forever as dark and bloody ground. The disappearance of some ugly watercolors wouldn't even make the cut on a list of bad things that had happened here.

But, damn it, I couldn't stop thinking about them. What could be behind the theft of nondescript old watercolors that no one had wanted since John's aunt's time? Could someone really have killed for them? Diane was in such a state I didn't know whether to believe anything she said or not. If I could just figure out what was behind all this.

Suddenly, I had it. Maybe the great rush of air sweeping down the lake and slicing like a tomahawk into my own brain cleared out the cobwebs and repaired some damaged synapses, but suddenly I had it. Diane had told me I could do anything I wanted with the painting. It was late now to call her. I went ahead on my own.

I rushed back inside and propped the painting against the couch with its back facing me. Heavy brown paper, surprisingly fresh looking once I'd brushed off a coat of dust, was glued to the back of the frame. I'd watched an artist friend frame her own paintings so many times I knew exactly what to do. I knelt down on the floor and used the nail file on my Swiss Army knife to work the brown paper loose. After a slow start I pulled it back easily. With the knife blade, I loosened the small triangular brads that held the next layer, a kind of thin board or masonite. When I lifted that out of the frame, I could see the back of the watercolor on fragile, dried out paper fitted tightly to the glass. I thought the masonite was only intended to hold the watercolor in place but, when I turned it around, I almost fell over backwards I was so shocked at what I saw. On canvas stretched over the board was a depiction of a flower, shockingly large and vibrant, the vivid reds of its petals, gashed by V's of yellow and lavender, soaring upward like flames. I didn't see a signature but it sure looked like a Georgia O'Keeffe to me.

I ran over to the computer and while I waited for it to dial into my server, I grabbed one of the library books and ran my finger down the index. No need. I was on the Internet in seconds. I'd already bookmarked a section on O'Keeffe paintings and I clicked onto it. Many of her paintings were included, ready to spring to life from the three dabs of color that always looked like happy faces to me in the corners of those little square frames. From my reading, I thought the one I'd found might be a Red Canna. I knew O'Keeffe had done several of them and I waited anxiously for the square to fill in. The colors came slowly. It was the same flower, but a more angular, geometric view.

I scrolled on. A few minutes later, miraculously, there it was, another Red Canna. As the colors flooded in, I recognized the painting that now stood in front of me on my living room floor. It was the very same painting, or one so much like it I couldn't distinguish between them. I was reeling with excitement but there was no one to share it with. I wanted to call Diane but it was so late and she'd been in such a state when she left, I decided against it. The painting had stayed hidden for over seventy years. One more day wasn't going to matter.

I spent the next hour jumping back and forth between the books and the Web sites, searching for information. During her time at Lake George O'Keeffe had begun filling the house with flowers, drawing inspiration for her paintings from the still life flower paintings of a French painter named Fantin Latour. His flowers were small, but by 1924 O'Keeffe was making hers huge. "People will be startled, they will have to look at them," she'd said. She was right; they did look and marveled at what they saw.

O'Keeffe's flowers were called soft and voluptuous; the colors, rapturous; the surfaces, enfolding and yielding. Her intent was to explore inner space, to lead one deep into the dark mysterious heart of the flower, the charged center of its being. I stopped reading and studied the painting I'd uncovered, willing it to lead me through its lush layers into its secret inner chambers. It was very erotic.

A slow tapping that I thought was the wind turned into a knock at the kitchen door. I looked out the window. Kevin stood there, his hair and long wool overcoat whipped about by the gale.

"You're home? It's so late," I said as I let him in.

"I drove straight through. I thought you'd be asleep but I decided to come by in case you were still up. When I saw your lights on..."

I grabbed him and pulled him inside, slamming the door against the wind. "Wait 'til you see this. You won't believe what I've found." I took celebratory beers out of the fridge for us and we sat on the sofa as I told him about the painting. I stood it on the floor across from where we were sitting and we both stared at it as I told my story.

For once Kevin didn't complain about my getting involved and heard me out without a protest. He was such a good listener; I could feel him recording and categorizing the information as I talked. At first, he asked all the obvious questions, the same ones I'd asked myself. Suddenly, he said, "Is it me or is this a very erotic painting, very sensual?" He slid his arm around my shoulders and pulled me toward him.

"Georgia O'Keeffe would not like to hear you say that," I told him as I riffled through one of the books on the sofa beside me. "It says here she was offended and surprised by accusations of sexuality."

"Really," he said. He leaned closer to me and ran his fingers slowly across my cheek. His hand was very cold but his fingers burned.

I put my own hand on top of his. "She would say your erotic vision is self-supplied." I said.

"Perhaps it is." He slid his forefinger back and forth across my lips.

"The technique she's using here is called magnification. She makes the flowers so large you have to see them," I said.

He brought his face close to mine. "Yes, I understand."

"The heart of the flower is dark and fragile, hidden from our sight," I said.

"Yes, I see that." He touched his lips to mine in his special way, kissing me gently as if I were the flower, as if he understood that my own heart -- itself dark and fragile and hidden -- could be easily broken.

We slid down together on the couch. I watched the painting as I moved against him. The colors, vibrant and pulsating, swirled in my head.

It was a long time before I felt like talking. I looked at the painting again. "Do you think we've been guilty of defiling great art?" I said.

He laughed, feeling around for his glasses which had somehow disappeared. "Defiling? No. Elevating it to the level of mythic experience, I'd say."

Had I been thinking of this guy as a backwoodsman? I must have been crazy.

THIRTEEN

The woman who answered my knock at her kitchen door that chilly Sunday afternoon was even older and more fragile than I'd expected. "Past eighty," Josie Donohue had said when she called to tell me she'd set up the interview I'd asked for, and Louise Cascadden, the expert on Georgia O'Keeffe, looked to be that age and more. White-haired, her slim body swaddled in a long cotton dress and apron, she held herself rigid, as if remaining upright required a tremendous effort of both body and will.

"Come in," she said as she admitted Josie and me. "I'm always delighted to find someone who wants to know about my favorite painter. We'll have tea while we talk."

Louise might appear delicate but I sensed an element of command in her statement. I shot Josie a warning glance. She'd made the arrangements for our visit without checking with me and I'd gone along. Now it was her turn to be agreeable. Whether she liked it or not, we were in for some serious tea drinking.

Louise Cascadden's home was doll house size, the entire downstairs all one room. She pointed us toward overstuffed chairs in a front corner. The furniture -- a Queen Ann sofa and the unmatched chairs we headed for -- had faded into a muted, homogenous group. The scarred tables completing the arrangement would have been described by antique dealers in my New York neighborhood as lovely old pieces.

"Sit down," Louise said as she went to stand behind the low counter that set off the kitchen from the rest of the room. "I'll just be a minute. It's such a coincidence that you've asked about O'Keeffe right now. Someone else expressed interest in her recently -- Edward Maranville, the man who was murdered. Did you know him?"

I shook my head. I hoped I wouldn't have to repeat my account of finding Edward's body to Louise -- and I didn't intend to tell anyone about the painting I'd found. Diane could decide how to handle that discovery. "He asked you about Georgia O'Keeffe? When was this?"

"Oh dear, I'm not sure. A couple of months ago. Asked Martin and me and everyone else he thought had any ties to O'Keeffe or the Stieglitz family. There aren't too many people left now with firsthand knowledge of them, you know."

"Yes, I suppose that's true." If Edward had questioned people, why had he and Bertholdt become so angry when Charles did the same thing?

Louise lifted the teakettle from the gas burner, shook it and set it back down. "You're planning an article, Josie tells me. Where will you place it?"

"I've done some features for the Post Standard. Or... Well, I'm not sure yet." I was afraid I'd jinx myself if I mentioned the Times.

Louise pointed at the little table next to where Josie was sitting. "I left some books there I thought you might be interested in."

Josie pulled one of the two large volumes onto her lap and began to leaf through it. "Awesome," she said.

"I've read about how Georgia came here with Stieglitz and stayed at his family's home," I said.

Louise nodded in agreement. "Yes. She spent summers here for a number of years, extended summers actually. She often stayed on into the fall, loved the autumn colors, the quiet after the summer people had left. Took short trips occasionally. She wanted to travel but Stieglitz didn't. She fell in love with New Mexico when she visited there in the late twenties. After a while she began spending her summers there."

"And finally made it her permanent home?"

"But not until after Stieglitz died. She was very devoted to him, you know, although she felt pressured at times. She commented that she couldn't live where she wanted to, do what she wanted to, even say what she wanted to."

"It's surprising to realize she felt that way, isn't it? I always think of her as such a free spirit," I said.

"She became one eventually, of course. A friend of ours recalls seeing Stieglitz and O'Keeffe walking to the village together every day. She was always referred to as O'Keeffe, never as Georgia. They both dressed entirely in black, you know, an unusual looking couple. People around here didn't know quite what to make of them, thought perhaps that was how all artists looked."

The teakettle emitted a low whistling sound. Louise shut off the gas and filled a silver teapot with the boiling water. She transferred the pot to a silver tray which already held cups and saucers and a delicate glass plate piled with pale golden cookies. I stood up and started toward her to help, but she waved me away. "No, no. I can manage. Be comfortable."

She crept in from the kitchen, holding the tray with the heavy tea service in front of her. I held my breath. I was sure she was going to collapse under its weight. She took the smallest steps I'd ever seen. Her feet were tiny, her insteps swollen over the vamp of her shoes. She set the tray on one of the low tables and began the long, slow pouring of our tea. A full-blown Japanese tea ceremony couldn't have taken longer. Josie, fortunately, was preoccupied with the book. I gritted my teeth and waited.

More minutes passed before Louise handed us each a cup of tea and offered the plate of lemon flavored cookies. "Perhaps you could start your article with Stieglitz's initial reaction to O'Keeffe's work. She was teaching in Texas, I believe, when her friend, Anita Pollitzer, sent him some of her drawings."

"I've read that," I said.

"So you know Stieglitz recognized O'Keeffe's genius at once, knew she was unique, an original. 'At last, a woman on paper,' is what he said."

Josie looked up in surprise. "That's the name of this book."

Louise smiled over at her. "Clever of Pollitzer to choose that as the title for her book, wasn't it?"

"Most appropriate," I said.

Josie went back to her reading.

"Stieglitz immediately arranged a show for her in his gallery at 291 Fifth Avenue," Louise continued. "He displayed her drawings without her permission, even got her name wrong. Called her Virginia O'Keeffe. She was enraged when she learned what he'd done. One of Martin's favorite images was of O'Keeffe hauling herself up in the gallery's rickety, hand-pulled elevator to tell him off."

"But he won her over very quickly, didn't he?" I asked.

"Yes. The romance developed soon after. He was twenty-three years her senior and married, but none of that mattered to them. They began living together and coming here summers, as you know."

"A friend told me she didn't care for this area, felt there was too much green."

Louise frowned, shaking her head at my comment. "I've never understood why people insist on emphasizing that particular remark. O'Keeffe loved the lake and the hills around it, said that after the nightmare of New York she could really breath here."

"She stayed at the Stieglitz family home?"

"Yes. At Oaklawn, and later at a place called Hill Cottage. Mrs. Stieglitz accepted her immediately and was very good to her, but the demands of a large household overwhelmed her."

"Weren't they well off enough to have servants?"

"They had one anyway -- a housekeeper, Margaret Prosser. She and O'Keeffe were very friendly, at least for a time. It's believed the relationship ended badly. Georgia O'Keeffe was probably not an easy person to stay friends with."

"What do you mean?" This was the kind of personal information I was looking for.

"She wanted to paint and suffered from the lack of privacy. Stieglitz was gregarious, you know, but she was a very private person. Wanted her own space, as the young people say now."

"And that was hard to find at Oaklawn?"

"Yes. Extended family. Many comings and goings. Sometimes Stieglitz would row her out on the lake at night so they could steal a few moments alone. There's one small piece O'Keeffe supposedly painted while sitting in the stern of a rowboat in the dark. Only about six by eight inches, quite different from her other lake paintings."

"She painted the lake frequently, I know. What else? Flowers?"

"A variety of subjects – skies, clouds, the trees, especially an old chestnut they both loved, and yes, she was into what she called her flower life by then. She began painting those enormous blooms that filled an entire canvas. She said she made them like huge buildings going up, but they were nothing like buildings.

They were lush and sensual, erotic even, although she never agreed with the critics who expressed opinions like that."

I felt my face get hot. I changed the subject quickly. "She was starting to develop her own style during her years here?"

"Yes, she said as long as she couldn't do as she wanted in other ways, she would be stupid not to paint as she wanted to, since it was nobody's business but her own. By her third summer here she'd fixed up a little building to work in. Called it the Shanty; got her own space that way."

"Are any of her paintings in museums around here?"

"Sadly, no. Not that I know of."

"Privately owned? Maybe even left around some place, perhaps forgotten, overlooked?"

Louise's tea cup made a little clatter as she set it back into the saucer. "I believe I understand what you're asking. Funny, Edward Maranville asked my husband almost the same question shortly before Martin died."

"Asked your husband about paintings O'Keeffe might have left behind here? What did he tell him?"

"Just what I'm about to tell you after I give you more tea."

"Thank you, no. But do go on with what you were saying."

"There have been rumors over the years about people with paintings in their possession, but nobody ever came forward. Martin and I never put much stock in those stories."

"But didn't I read paintings of O'Keeffe's turned up in Texas few years ago, paintings hidden for more than seventy years?"

"You're speaking of the watercolors referred to as Canyon Suite, I believe. When O'Keeffe was teaching in Texas, she gave a student named Ted Reid twenty-eight of her watercolors. He kept them hidden away, wrapped in brown paper, all his life. Apparently never told his wife and family about them. They came into his granddaughter's possession after his death."

"Perhaps something similar happened here."

"Oh, no. That was entirely different. Reid was O'Keeffe's friend, probably something more than a friend. She supposedly gave him the watercolors before he left for World War I. She was very careful about her work. There's a well-documented story about her tossing paintings into a wood burning stove when she was young, saying she didn't want them floating around to haunt her when she became famous."

"You think there's no chance..."

"One very slim possibility which Martin and I didn't find particularly believable. It's been said she once asked a housekeeper -- whether it was Margaret or not, I don't know -- to destroy paintings for her and the woman didn't do it. Smuggled them out of the house and gave them to a friend to keep for her."

"So couldn't the friend be another Ted Reid?"

"No. Martin and I felt we'd arrived at a thorough understanding of O'Keeffe through our research. Neither of us believed she would have asked someone else to destroy her work. If she wanted something done, she took care of it."

"But it's a possibility though, isn't it?" I persisted. Maybe John's aunt was the friend who'd been asked to keep the paintings.

Louise shook her head. "No, no. The story is pure rumor. Like Georgie, our lake monster -- you've heard of him haven't you? He surfaces once in a while but the sighting always turns out to be a figment of someone's imagination or, at most, an amusing hoax."

I still refused to give up. "But you said Edward Maranville questioned your husband about lost paintings. Did Edward give your husband any special reason why he was asking?"

"I suppose he'd heard the rumors just as you have. Martin agreed to make some inquiries for him. They were going to talk further, but then Martin had his accident."

An icy draft came out of nowhere and sent a cold chill rippling down my spine. "Accident?"

"Automobile. He was killed on this road, driving down to the village. Apparently, his brakes failed. He pulled out onto the highway without stopping -- not like Martin at all -- and a truck hit him. Hit him right on the driver's side." She bit down on her lower lip, her face twisted in pain as she struggled to regain her composure.

"I'm so sorry. I didn't know." My mind was racing full tilt. Edward Maranville. Martin Cascadden. Two men had been inquiring about the rumors of lost O'Keeffe paintings. Now, both men were dead.

Louise pushed herself up out of the chair. "Dear Martin. It's been more than two months now and I still can't believe he's gone. We can talk another day when you have more time."

But I have time now, I wanted to tell her. There was so much more I needed to find out, but I could see she was too shaken to go on.

Louise turned away from me, heading quickly toward the kitchen, the fastest I'd seen her move. As she tottered along, the delicate China cup trembled and rattled in its saucer. Suddenly, it fell in a slow, lazy arc to the floor. The small Oriental it landed on had been lovely once but now, like everything else in this sad little house, it was worn with age, unable to cushion the cup's fall. The cup shattered into a dozen pieces.

I bent quickly to pick up the shards of china. As I gathered them into my hands, Louise hovered over me, pale as a wraith in the gathering dusk.

FOURTEEN

Josie and I said little to each other as we left Louise Cascadden's house and climbed into my van. We both stared straight ahead, prisoners of our own thoughts. Josie might crack wise but underneath her carefully tended veneer she was softhearted and I suspected she'd been as moved by Louise's circumstances as I'd been.

The view as we descended the steep, winding road down the mountain took my mind off the visit -- at least for a time. Many of the trees had already shed their leaves and, below us, I could see a long stretch of lake glowing in the light of the setting sun. The three peninsulas at its southern end with their honeycomb of bays and coves jutted out into the glistening water. I thought of the painting O'Keeffe had called Lake George With Crows. In her mind's eye, she'd seen the lake from above, as we saw it now, but she'd tilted its plane upward and painted it as a dark ovoid, accented with the darker outlines of three crows taking flight over its waters. The lake had proved a wonderful subject for her -- she'd presented it lovingly, in many different ways, capturing its moods, letting her own imagination take flight.

The narrow road twisted and turned; at times the drop was alarmingly steep. More than once, as I navigated a hairpin turn, I found myself staring into empty space. The mix of beauty and fear was exhilarating.

The mountain road ended without warning and the merge with the highway was quick and dangerous. Louise's words came rushing back. I pictured Martin pumping brakes that didn't respond, charging out into traffic, unable to stop his car. I shuddered as I glanced to my left, half expecting to see a tractor trailer bearing down on us out of a blind curve.

Josie expressed my unspoken thoughts. "Jeez, the poor old guy probably never knew what hit him."

"I was thinking the same thing. This is a bad spot," I said.

"People thought there was something weird about the accident, but it's easy to see how you could get clobbered here."

"What do you mean -- weird?"

"They say Mr. C. was a real fuddy duddy. Drove slow, stopped and looked both ways before he pulled out, like a little kid crossing the street. Nobody understood how the accident could have happened -- at least not to him."

"But Louise said his brakes failed."

"Nah. Jake talked to the guys in the garage. His brakes were all right. I guess it makes Louise feel better to think that's what happened."

For the second time that afternoon an icy hand massaged the back of my neck, sending shivers of fear down my spine.

As I was dropping Josie off, Kate ran out of the house. "Ellen, I've been watching for you. Come in and have dinner with us," she called.

The invitation couldn't have been more welcome. I

practically threw myself off the high seat of the van. The aromas wafting out of Kate's kitchen made me think I'd died and gone to heaven.

"I've made a chicken and rice dish. I hope you'll like it," she said.

"I like it already," I told her.

Josie prowled around the kitchen, stopping to uncover a casserole on top of the stove and a pan of something simmering on one of the burners. She screwed up her face. "Not this crap."

"You like that recipe. You ate two helpings the last time I made it," Kate said.

"Oh, Mom, that's what you always say. I'm not hungry anyway. I'm going upstairs." Josie tossed her jacket on a kitchen chair and flounced out.

I stared after her in surprise. "She was great with Louise Cascadden. She must have used up all her good will over there."

Kate picked up the jacket from the chair and hung it on a hook by the back door. "No, it's me. She feels duty bound to treat me like dirt. Don't ask me why. Maybe I should serve her a hot dog on a fork. Didn't you say that was one of your mother's specialties?"

"Do it. It would be fun to see her reaction. But keep in mind that's one of the things I hold against my mother. Of course, if I thought I'd treated her the way Josie treats you sometimes, I'd stop blaming her for a lot of things."

"Josie will get over it eventually, I expect." Kate unwrapped the paper from the top of a wine bottle and twisted a corkscrew into the cork. She pressed the chrome arms down; the cork slid up with a little pop. "We must talk only of cheerful things so you can enjoy my casserole. Tell me about your visit with Mrs. Cascadden."

"Not much to cheer you there, I'm afraid, but I would like to get your reaction." I described the conversation with Louise and the way she'd suddenly cut short the visit.

Kate listened attentively as she served our food, nodding but saying little. "I'm sure she's devastated by her husband's death. You'll call her again, won't you, get her to talk with you another time?"

Josie, true to her word, ignored Kate when she shouted up the stairs that dinner was ready. Although Kate glanced toward the hall several times, she didn't call her daughter again. "I'm trying to go along with her on things that don't really matter and save my big guns for important issues," she explained.

I didn't comment but I understood Kate's disappointment. She loved preparing a special meal, saw her food as a gift of love. By refusing to eat with us Josie had found an effective way to hurt her. The girl was pleasant enough to me -- most of the time anyway. Why did she feel obliged to keep up a running battle with her mother?

Over dinner Kate and I fell into our usual easy exchange. She liked to discuss her plans for her catering business with me, urging me to describe parties I'd attended in New York, always searching for new ideas. In turn, I enjoyed her chatter about Lake George. Her observations on the town and the people in it were funny and perceptive.

"Any chance you know where Diane is this weekend?" I asked at one point. "I've left messages on her machine but she hasn't called back."

"She probably went to visit her son. She does that once in a while, gets a motel room near his school and spends time with him. I imagine she'll be back tomorrow.

"Trying to put some distance between herself and John maybe. She's really upset with him right now."

I expected Kate, always supportive of Diane, to lash out against John, but she surprised me. "I try not to take sides in their problems. Diane and I have been friends for years but John's been a good friend to me too."

"Really?" What did that mean, I wondered.

Kate picked up on my curiosity. "No deep, dark secrets," she said, laughing. "John's saved me from making some costly mistakes with my business. Never lets me pay him for his advice. I'm really indebted to him."

We cleared the table. Kate produced an apple pie that could have made the cover of Gourmet Magazine and while we lingered over pie and coffee, the doorbell rang. Michael, Kevin's eight-year-old, bounded in with Kevin following close behind. He was carrying Connor.

"What is it, Connor? Don't you feel good?" Kate asked the little boy. She felt his forehead, gave Kevin a concerned glance, then extended her arms to the child. He went to her willingly and snuggled his flushed face into her neck.

"He's a little under the weather." Kevin nodded at Kate and signaled me to follow him into the hall. Kate sat down on the couch, rocking Connor gently in her arms.

As soon as we were outside the door, Kevin said, "I've been looking for you. We went by your place to say hello and saw a car parked at the end of your driveway. It pulled away fast when I showed up. Looked like somebody had been staking out your camp. I didn't like it."

"You didn't recognize the car?"

"Big, dark blue car. It might have been a rental plate. I wondered if it was Tim."

My ex-fiancé reduced to stalking me? "No, that's not like him. Could it have been Diane Anderson? I've been trying to get in touch with her all weekend."

"No. It wasn't her car anyway. Who else knows Diane brought that painting to you?"

"Nobody, as far as I know. She was adamant about keeping it a secret. And remember, she didn't know the O'Keeffe painting was underneath the other one."

"But somebody else did."

I really didn't want to think about that. "Could it have been John Anderson you saw? Diane swore he'd find the painting if she took it to her condo. I thought she was exaggerating, but maybe she was right."

"Not a car I've seen him drive, but..."

"He saw me at Diane's condo the morning after we found the body. If he discovered she took the painting, then checked her condo and didn't find it, maybe he would think of me next."

"That theory's a bit far fetched. Still, I'd rather believe it was John snooping around than someone else."

I tried to lighten things up a little. "He gets my vote. He's a CPA, remember? Putting two and two together is his specialty."

He made a face at me, then reached out and touched my cheek in an affectionate gesture, something he seldom did when his boys were nearby. "Joke if you want to, but I don't like this at all."

As we walked back to the living room, Josie clattered down the stairs. "Hey, you guys," she yelled, her good humor restored. She reached into a drawer of the desk for a deck of cards. "Come 'ere, Michael, I'll play you a game of Crazy Eights."

Michael rushed over to her and watched her deal out the cards. Connor made a half-hearted effort to get off Kate's lap, then sank back against her.

"He's got another ear infection, I'm afraid," Kevin said. "I've got a call in for the doctor. The boys are staying with me tonight. Lisa went away for the weekend and she's not coming back until tomorrow."

Kate offered dinner or dessert, but Kevin refused.

"We've got to get home. I think we'll need to get a prescription filled." He picked up Connor and settled him against his shoulder.

As Kevin started for the door, Connor reached out to me. His soft little hand felt dry and hot when I took it in mine. I put it to my lips and kissed it. "I hope you get better real fast," I said.

"Thank you, Ellen," he said so sweetly I wanted to grab him and hug him to me.

At the door Kevin paused for a minute. "I was thinking I'd call the sheriff and ask them to check your place out."

"And tell them what -- that you saw a car there? They'd think you were crazy. And you couldn't mention the painting, you know. Diane wanted to talk to John about it and I promised I'd give her a couple of days to work things out."

Kevin made one last attempt. "I'm wasting my breath, I know, but I wish you'd stay here tonight. Kate would be glad to have you and I'd sure feel more comfortable."

"Nonsense, I'll be fine," I told him. And as I walked back into Kate's cozy living room, I was sure I would be.

FIFTEEN

An hour later on my drive back to the cove my score on the bravery scale plummeted. The overcast fall night was especially dark with no sign of moon or stars. As I left Lake George Village and headed south along Route 9, I realized that all the places I passed -- motels, gas stations, convenience stores and restaurants that bustled with activity in the summer -- were closed tight, either for the season or for the night, their outer lights shut off, their windows blank and staring. I felt like a character in a sci fi movie after everyone else has been abducted by aliens, rushing headlong into some terrible, unseen danger.

When I reached Cove Road, I saw lights in some of the houses but the doors were shut tight; the inhabitants, most of them elderly, sequestered inside. Once again, as I drove down the macadam drive to the lake, I realized how remote my uncle's camp was. I'd lived and worked for years in a city teeming with people; now I was the only person staying on this deserted stretch of lakeshore. Even after I turned the van's heater up to high, I couldn't stop shivering.

I gave myself a good talking to. If someone had been checking out the place while I was gone, it must have been John Anderson. Diane was probably right about him. He'd found out she'd taken the painting and somehow he'd traced it to me. John Anderson was a professional with a position in the community -- nobody to be afraid of. If he wanted the painting back, he'd knock on my door and ask for it.

I parked the van and sat for several minutes, scanning the area for cars, prowlers, signs of anything out of the ordinary. Ominous, dark shapes loomed along the edge of the lake. The leafless branches of the maple in my uncle's yard rubbed together, emitting mournful creakings in counterpoint to the sighing of the wind and the relentless pound of the waves against the shore. Because I'd expected to be home before dark, I'd failed to leave the outside light turned on. I wouldn't make that mistake again. My peace of mind was worth adding a little extra to my electric bill.

When I'd satisfied myself no one was around, I made a fist with my keys sticking out between my fingers and walked quickly to the back door. Nobody jumped me. I unlocked the door and swung inside, switching on both the outside and kitchen lights.

I heaved a sigh, actually a half sign. My relief at being safe inside with the door locked behind me lasted less than five seconds. Someone had been in the camp while I was out. I knew it immediately. Creepy feelings slid along my nerves, setting off a full-sized ice-cube-down-the-spine sensation. I moved slowly through the rooms, noting the telltale signs -- a chair moved away from the kitchen table when I remembered pushing it in, books piled on the round table in the living room with one on top I knew I hadn't left on top. Somebody had been in here, poking through my stuff.

I picked up the phone and called Kevin. "You were right to be suspicious about that car you saw. Somebody's been in the camp."

"Get out. Do it right now. Go to Kate's and stay overnight. I can't come over there," he said.

"I know you can't. I don't expect you to. Whoever it was is gone now. There's no sign of a car outside, no lights on in here. I'm not going to Kate's. I just want you to stay on the line while I look around and make sure the painting's still here."

I carried my new portable phone with me as I climbed the stairs. I did a quick check of my bedroom. Nobody hiding there, everything in its proper place. In the small bedroom where I'd hidden the painting, nothing had been disturbed. I'd arranged the painting just so in the sagging middle of the old bed. I could see the contour of its frame outlined under the bedspread exactly as I'd left it. I'd draped a spare blanket across the bed -- artfully, I'd thought -- to camouflage the edges of the painting. It was even harder to spot than I remembered.

"No problem," I said into the phone. "It's right where I left it. Sorry to have bothered you. How's Connor? I hope I didn't wake him."

"I'm keeping him up anyway. The pharmacist's dropping off a prescription on his way home. Once I get that down him, he should be able to sleep. But, Ellen..."

"No more. I'm fine. Call me tomorrow if you get a chance." I turned off the phone fast before he could argue and went back downstairs. The painting had been right where I'd hidden it. I'd outfoxed John Anderson. Now, all I had to do was wait for Diane to get home. Once she did, I'd insist she take the painting back and make up her mind what she was going to do with it.

Relieved, I sauntered into the kitchen and opened the refrigerator door. Maybe a cold drink... Suddenly every nerve in my body coiled into a tight knot. I pushed the door closed and swung around with my back against it.

A tall, nervous looking man in urgent need of a shave stood in the middle of my kitchen. He jabbed a very black, very hideous gun in my direction. “I believe you have something that belongs to me and I want it returned immediately.”

I jumped back so hard the handle of the refrigerator stabbed into my spine Thanks to a former boyfriend, I recognized the gun as a .22, not the biggest handgun maybe, but deadly enough to do serious damage, especially at this close range. Could this be the vagrant they’d been talking about at the restaurant -- except this time he was armed with a gun instead of a knife?

“You have something of mine and I want it,” he said again. His wild-eyed, desperate look was as frightening as the gun.

I forced myself to take a deep breath, although sucking air into my lungs turned out to be harder than I thought it would be. The intruder was a complete stranger to me; I was sure I’d never seen him before. His clothes were rumpled and soiled, but they fit well and they’d cost plenty. I’d seen enough homeless wandering the New York streets to know this guy wasn’t a vagrant. I went on the offensive. “What the hell are you doing in my house? You almost scared me to death.”

“You’ve got my painting and I want it.” He thrust the gun toward me again. His hand shook so violently I was afraid he’d shoot me whether he meant to or not.

“Well then, put that gun down and tell me who you are.”

“Never mind who I am. Just give me my painting and I’ll leave.”

“Did John Anderson send you?” I demanded.

“Of course not. And also, give me your car keys. I don’t have transportation right now.” The intruder uttered a high, mirthless cackle that did nothing to reassure me about his emotional state.

"I'm not giving you anything until you tell me who you are." It was a bluff, but to my surprise, he folded his cards.

"I'm Edward Maranville and you've got a painting that belongs to me."

"Don't tell me that. Edward Maranville's dead."

"You have Diane Anderson to thank for that bit of misinformation."

"But I'm the one who found your body."

"Correction: you found a body. Fortunately for me, it wasn't mine."

"You mean Diane was wrong? Whose body was it then? Where have you been since last Sunday? Why haven't you gone to the sheriff?" I rattled off the questions as fast as they popped into my mind, and I still had plenty more to ask.

Edward Maranville stopped me with another wave of his gun. "I assume you've heard the expression, 'curiosity killed the cat.' Never mind the third degree or that's what's going to happen to you."

I spread out my hands and patted the air in front of me in what I hoped was a calming gesture. "Mr. Maranville, you don't want to kill me. You want me to give you the painting and I'm more than willing to do that. I didn't want to be involved in this crazy mess in the first place. I just wanted to interview you about Georgia O'Keeffe."

"Yes, we can still do that," he said to my astonishment, "but right now, you must give me the painting. Don't try to tell me it's not here because I know it is."

I kept my voice low and spoke in the calmest tones I could manage. "I'll get it for you."

My choice of words set him off again. "Oh, no. Don't try to go anywhere without me. I'm staying with you. Lead the way."

With Edward trailing close behind me, I walked slowly into the living room and pointed toward the stairs. Whether the painting belonged to him or not, I saw no reason not to give it to him. He was threatening to shoot me, for God sake; I didn't need any better reason than that for going along with him. Still, what if he decided to kill me after he got the painting? I considered that possibility on the long, slow climb up the stairs. My legs felt as if they might give out any minute but I made it to the top and led him into the small bedroom. I pointed to the outline of the frame under the bedspread.

"Thank heaven, I've found it." He pulled a handkerchief out of his pocket with his free hand and wiped away the beads of sweat trickling down his face.

I pushed the blanket aside. I flipped back the bedspread with a quick, fluid motion, almost as if I were unveiling an O'Keeffe at the Met. I heard a horrified gasp. I didn't know if it came from Edward Maranville or from me or from both of us simultaneously. We stood side by side, both in a state of shock, staring down at the bed. The only thing under the spread was the cover from a large cardboard box, placed exactly where I'd left the painting, its turned-up edges the very same size as the frame. I even recognized the cover. It had been taken off a box of my aunt's old household items which were stored in the little space under the eaves at the side of the bedroom. Such a clever move. If it hadn't been for Edward, I would never have suspected the painting was missing until I went to return it to Diane.

Several things happened at once. Edward and I both leaned forward to get a better look, as if a closer inspection would change what we were seeing. Edward, ignoring the obvious, lifted the box cover and the bedding and began poking around in the bed. I swooped down fast and yanked the gun out of his hand.

I stepped back from the bed, thrusting the gun at him the same way he'd jabbed it at me. I tried to sound gruff and sure of myself. "Now, I've got the gun and

I'm not afraid to use it."

"Oh dear, oh dear, why did you go and do that? I wasn't really going to shoot you." He staggered backward away from me and collapsed on a chair, holding his head in his hands.

"How was I supposed to know that? Well, I'm the one with the gun now and somebody's beat you to the painting. I'm calling the sheriff."

Edward's face turned even grayer under his stubble. "Don't do that. We don't need to involve law enforcement agencies. Just tell me the truth about the painting. Had you really put it in that bed?"

"Yes, that's where I hid it. Whoever took it was very shrewd. I checked the bed when I came in and I thought everything was just as I left it."

"This is awful, just awful. I've got to get that painting back. It's promised to someone, someone who's not going to like this development at all. You've got to help me."

This man didn't lack for nerve. "Excuse me? I've got to help you?"

"I'm in a terrible mess. I haven't eaten all day. I'm cold and exhausted and I don't know where my car is and I've got to find that painting.

"You picked a poor way to go about it. I'm turning you in." I held the gun on him and pointed him down the stairs.

"No, don't do that. Please. Give me one more day. I'll find Diane. She'll help me. I promise I'll clear everything up and go to the sheriff myself tomorrow."

"No way," I reached for the phone.

"Wait. You wanted to know about Georgia O'Keeffe. I'll give you the interview of your life. I can tell you things that will make your head spin -- and your readers' heads too. I'll call you from Diane's tomorrow, I swear I will. You'll sell your feature for more money than you've ever been paid for an article before."

I wouldn't have to sell it for much to be paid more than I'd ever been paid before, but I didn't tell him that. Instead, even though I'd been burned on that call-you-tomorrow line many times before in my life, I stood there with the phone in my hand, listening to the dial tone, while Edward Maranville scurried out my kitchen door and disappeared up the drive into the darkness.

SIXTEEN

When I came downstairs the next morning, the sun had popped up behind French Mountain, trailing what looked like a spectacular fall day behind it. Ordinarily, the light and color pouring into the camp would have sent my spirits soaring. But my experience with Edward had left me shaken. I'd slept poorly, tormented by the thought that I'd been wrong to let him leave without calling the sheriff.

To add to my discomfort, the temperature had nose-dived during the night. The chill drafts along the floor gave me my first real taste of what an Adirondack winter would be like. As I started my coffee, I could hear Ray's old oil furnace wheezing away in the cellar, trying desperately to send up some heat.

With the furnace straining so hard, I didn't pick up at first on the sporadic rustlings from the front porch. Strange creakings I couldn't identify told me someone or something was out there, but the living room windows were glazed with frost and I couldn't see through them. I reached into the closet for an old winter coat of

Ray's, heavier than anything I'd brought with me, and put it on. I slid open the desk drawer, took out the gun I'd hidden there the night before and slipped it into a pocket. Then, I eased open the front door and stepped out onto the porch. The wind came whipping down the lake straight from the North Pole.

The only thing left on the porch for the winter was an old metal glider too heavy and cumbersome to be moved to the cellar for storage. I'd put away the cushions and covered the frame with the canvas glider cover just the way Ray had told me to do. Now, I stared down at one of the strangest sights I'd ever seen. Edward Maranville, a candidate for hypothermia if I ever saw one, was curled up in a fetal position on the steel springs of the glider, clutching the canvas cover he'd tried unsuccessfully to wrap around himself. I kept my right hand on the gun in my pocket and called his name again and again. There was no response. I shook his arm almost out of its socket before he finally stirred and struggled to a sitting position

Despite what we've been led to believe by movies and television, a man waking up in the morning is often not a pretty sight -- or sound -- even under the best of circumstances. And these circumstances were definitely not the best. Edward was slight of build but he was close to six feet tall, so he must have been mighty uncomfortable scrunched up on that glider. He didn't make eye contact with me at first, but concentrated on rubbing the circulation back into his legs, accompanying his slaps with a lot of groaning and hawking. His beard was even scruffier than it had been the evening before and his thinning hair looked as if someone had taken a eggbeater to it. I couldn't help feeling sorry for him, not a logical reaction when I remembered how he'd threatened me with a gun.

"Please let me come in and get cleaned up," he begged, "and I'll give you that interview on Georgia O'Keeffe right now. You didn't call the sheriff, did you?"

What can I tell you? The flesh is weak. I wanted that interview bad. I showed Edward to the bathroom, located a disposable razor and a new toothbrush and left him to shower. By the time he came downstairs, clean and freshly shaven but in the same crumpled clothing he'd apparently been wearing for days, I'd poured orange juice and whipped eggs for an omelet. He gobbled up the omelet along with a stack of toast and everything else I brought out. Finally, just shy of emptying my refrigerator and larder completely, he heaved a huge sigh and said he'd had enough.

"I've kept my part of the bargain. Now you keep yours," I said, planting myself in a chair across from him. "Tell me the truth about the painting I found. Was it a genuine Georgia O'Keeffe?"

I skewered him with my sternest look and spoke in my best no-nonsense voice. I expected a good return on my investment. I'd not only have the devil of a time explaining my actions to Kevin -- maybe to Jack Whittemore as well if I was really unlucky -- but I'd just used up a big share of my week's groceries on this guy.

Edward leaned back in his chair and waved me silent. "Art has a threefold grip on me," he intoned as if he were addressing a full lecture hall. "First, more than most people, I understand its value as an investment. My family's fortune was secured by art. I've been forced to sell some of our finest pieces simply to survive. Not to live as I once lived, you understand, as my parents lived in those halcyon days before the war, days I only dimly remember, but merely to survive."

I found my thinking steered in a totally different direction. "Do you mean the missing painting was once part of your family's collection?" I didn't see how it could have been but...

"No, no, of course not. I'm talking about my family in Romania. They had taste, discernment, they skimmed the cream of European art, magnificent old masters, innovative newcomers like the Fauves, always the best. They knew nothing of O'Keeffe, but I'm sure they would have recognized the quality of her work, her genius."

"Did someone give you that painting or sell it to you?" I was well-mannered enough not to use the word steal to a breakfast guest.

"The painting is mine, I'm proud to tell you. This is the second way art has enslaved me. Its esthetic impact overwhelms me. For some people it's great music, you know; for me it's art. Its spirit possesses me, transforms me. Like La Belle Dame sans Merci it holds me in its thrall.".

I'd been an English major in college. I loved it when people spun out literary allusions like that. But Diane and Tom had been right about this guy -- he could talk you into the ground. I thrust out my hand in an emphatic stop signal and restated my question slowly and deliberately. "Was that painting an authentic Georgia O'Keeffe?"

"You saw it, didn't you? The Red Canna? You saw how she presented her flowers -- open mouthed, silky skinned, the folds, the fissures, the labial curves And those colors. Kandinsky said colors directly affect the soul. She understood that. What she created wasn't a male view of female sexuality; she actually showed us the feelings of an open, receptive woman."

I felt the blood rush to my face. I'd not only seen that, I'd felt it, understood it. Perhaps I couldn't have put my feelings into those words, but I too had been possessed, transformed by something very powerful.

For the first time Edward looked directly at me. "I'm embarrassing you. Your face is as red as the canna. Is it because the emotions she awakened in you run so deep or are you afraid to face them?"

"Yes. No. I..."

"I recall something one reviewer said of O'Keeffe's work: It's the universe we're looking at. You take a seed and unroll the cosmos out of it. That is the essence."

I was in deep now, over my head. I wanted him to keep talking, but he was losing me. If I'd only had my tape recorder set up. Someone knocked on the back door. Glad of a diversion, I went to open it. Diane Anderson stood there, her hand raised, ready to knock again.

My annoyance with her came boiling up. "Diane, I've tried so many times to reach you. Why didn't you let me know if you were going out of town?"

Diane gaped at me as if I'd gone mad, then pushed past me into the kitchen. Every trace of color drained from her face. She reeled backward, reaching out an arm to steady herself against the door. "Who... Who is that?"

Edward got up immediately and went to her, trying to draw her into a hug. "It's me, Diane. I'm very much alive."

Diane jerked away from him. She raised her hands to her mouth as her eyes filled with tears. "What have I done? I've made a terrible mistake."

"Really. Is the fact you made a mistake the primary issue here? At the very least, you could act glad to see me." Edward sniffed with annoyance and backed away from her.

Diane sank down on a chair next to me and I started on a convoluted account of what had happened since she dropped off the painting. When I described finding the Red Canna hidden behind the watercolor, she let out a shriek.

"You're telling me you found a genuine Georgia O'Keeffe painting underneath my watercolor? I don't believe it. Then, the others in the closet probably were O'Keeffe paintings too. They must be the missing paintings people talk about. They've got to be worth a fortune. Ellen, you've found a gold mine. You're wonderful." She threw her arms around me, almost yanking me off my chair.

"But the painting's gone, Diane. Someone's stolen it."

Once again she stared at me with shocked disbelief. Then a quick turnaround. "What? What are you saying? How could that have happened? Ellen, I expected you to keep it safe for me."

"Oh no, you didn't," I said quickly. "You told me to throw it in the lake if I wanted to. When I found the flower painting underneath the watercolor, I knew it might be valuable. I found a good hiding place for it, at least I thought I had." I'd actually started enumerating some of the other hiding places I'd considered before I came to my senses and stopped myself. I shouldn't have to explain or apologize. Let Diane apologize to me for dragging me into this mess.

"You mean the painting's gone. I can't believe it," she said.

"Somebody must have known it was here. And whoever took it was very clever. I wouldn't have missed it if Edward hadn't come calling."

Edward shifted in his chair, but said nothing, making no effort to restate his earlier claim of ownership.

"I've tried to call you a dozen times, Diane," I went on. "I didn't want to go to the authorities until I'd talked to you. I figure the painting belongs to you. Your friend Edward seems to think differently."

Edward continued pouting, still not making any comment.

Diane swept her hair back with a quick, nervous gesture. "What authorities are you talking about? I would hope you wouldn't involve the sheriff."

Before I could ask why not, the phone rang. Kevin didn't waste time on hello. "Ellen, are you all right? I've been all this time waiting for the sitter. She had to get her own kids off to school before she could sit with Connor. He's better, but I decided to keep him home today."

There was a question about me in there somewhere, wasn't there? "I'm fine," I said.

"You don't sound fine, Ellen. What's going on?" Kevin said.

He wanted reassurance, but I was in no mood to give it. "Diane's here. I can't talk now. Don't worry. I'm all right."

As soon as I hung up, I lifted the filter out of the coffee maker and dumped the soggy grounds into the garbage. I rummaged in the cupboard for a new filter, then scooped out coffee for another pot. I had a feeling we were going to need it.

Diane turned her attention to Edward; her face twisted into an angry scowl. "Listen to me, Edward, I have a right to know. What happened at my summerhouse? Who was the dead man on the floor, the one I thought was you? I didn't look close enough at his face because it was burned so horribly I thought I was going to faint. Who was it?" Her voice, strident and angry, seemed to fill the small kitchen.

Edward spoke slowly, as if he'd memorized the words. "Diane, I don't know. I'd gone out for the evening. When I got to the front door, I saw someone had tried to start a fire in your living room. I could see the fire had gone out, but I panicked. I never went back inside. I didn't know anyone had been killed until the next day."

The falseness in his tone, the obviously rehearsed account made me sure he was lying. I chimed in with Diane. "Come on, Edward, you must have some idea who the man was. How do we know you didn't kill him?"

"I assure you I don't know anything about the man except that he was very, very unlucky. Somebody knew I was staying in your summerhouse, Diane, and went there to kill me. Instead they killed him by mistake and tried to burn the place down."

"Is that what you think happened, Edward?" I asked.

"Of course. That's why I've been hiding out this week. I'm afraid to go home to my own house. I don't know who I can trust. Once the murderer finds out I'm still alive, he may try again."

"Do you have enemies trying to kill you, Edward, or do you think the murderer was after the paintings?" I asked.

"Paintings? What paintings are you talking about?" Edward said.

Why was taking this tack? He'd insisted the painting upstairs was his; now he refused to claim it in front of Diane. I didn't understand this guy at all.

Diane ignored his question. "No, I'm sure John's taken the paintings. He's probably known all along what they were. I'm not going to let him get away with this. The summerhouse and its contents are half mine. That means those paintings are half mine too."

"But Diane, if John knew, why would he have kept them hidden all this time? It doesn't make sense," I said.

"I asked what paintings you're referring to, Diane?" Edward said. For a man who acted whiney he could sure sound mean.

"Don't play your silly games with me, Edward. You know very well what paintings -- the ones in the closet upstairs. You even looked at them for me years ago when I wanted them appraised. Ellen and I went to the summerhouse the other day and found only one of them left in that closet. I asked her to keep it for me. If that painting was really done by Georgia O'Keeffe, the others probably were too. There are a dozen or more missing. Ellen knows. Don't you, Ellen?" Diane looked to me for confirmation

I shrugged, suddenly aware I had no real proof other paintings existed, only Diane's word and the rows of tracks in the dust.

"John's managed to get them all somehow. He always gets everything he wants."

Edward gave her a disgusted look. "Your judgment tends to be clouded, Diane. We've talked about this before. You blame John for everything that goes wrong in your life. It's about time you got beyond that."

Diane clenched her teeth and glowered at him, ready to explode with rage, but Edward wasn't fazed. He glared back at her across the kitchen table.

I picked up the fresh pot of coffee. "Hey, you guys, how about we go for a real caffeine buzz? Want one last cup before you leave?"

Neither of them answered me. That's the trouble with subtle hints. Sometimes they're too subtle to make your point.

SEVENTEEN

The guests who wouldn't leave. Everyone's experienced that phenomenon, I suppose, and on that particular Monday morning it was my turn. Diane and Edward sat glued to their chairs, as if determined to outwait each other, and nothing I said or did seemed likely to change their minds. In my job as an outplacement counselor I'd hammered out a good many compromises -- but I couldn't get those two to budge from their respective positions.

"I'm telling you, Edward, those paintings are mine, at least half mine, and I'm entitled to my share," Diane said, slamming her hand down hard on the table.

"And as I've been telling you, Diane, you'd best discuss that matter with your ex-husband." Edward's precise, mincing way of speaking and his condescending tone ratcheted her anger up higher and higher until bright red blotches appeared on her face and she began to shake with frustration.

Diane continued to storm at him but Edward remained unruffled, refusing to be drawn into an argument. His supercilious smile would have enraged Mother Teresa.

I tried taking a stronger stand. "Listen, you two, you're not getting anywhere here and you're keeping me from my work. Diane, why don't you go and talk with John, see what he has to say about all this. Edward, I'll give you a ride to the Municipal Center and you can tell your story to Jack Whittemore."

Edward turned the full force of his condescension on me. "My dear young woman, despite what I may have implied last evening, going to the sheriff is not a viable alternative for me at this time. Those country bumpkins could easily conclude I did the murder and toss me into their jail. I can't go to my own home in case the murderer is lying in wait for me there. And I can't go back to Diane's."

Diane bristled. "Indeed you can't. You're not welcome there, I can assure you of that."

My suggestion, however, gave them something to agree on. They both hated it -- at least the part about involving Jack Whittemore. Diane was willing to question John about the missing paintings, but she shared Edward's view that neither he nor anyone else should contact the sheriff's investigator.

With one area of agreement reached, Diane and Edward softened a little toward one another and, after some prodding by me, worked out a plan of action. Diane would drive Edward to a motel where he could stay out of sight for a few more days. Then, she'd head for John's office and demand to know if he'd taken the paintings.

"Good thinking. Works for me." I jumped up from my chair and stood by the kitchen door. I pulled the door open and began fanning it back and forth.

Finally, they took the hint.

Once my guests were gone, I wasted no time getting to work. I was deep into my O'Keeffe research when Diane called to report. The first places she and

Edward had checked out were already closed for the winter but eventually they'd happened on the Tumbling Brook Motel, a collection of mismatched cabins halfway up a mountain north of Lake George Village. Edward hadn't warmed to the accommodations, but at that point he was desperate enough to take a room. He'd instructed Diane to tell me I could come there to continue the interview if I wanted to.

"Wait 'til you see that motel." Diane chuckled, making no effort to hide the satisfaction in her voice. "He's found a perfect spot to hide out in, but it's a Class A dump."

"Not Edward's usual style, I take it," I said. But I wasn't about to feel sorry for him. Anything had to be better than his night on my glider. I went back to my books -- or tried to.

Josie Donohue arrived less than ten minutes later, practically skipping across the kitchen floor in her excitement. Electrical current hummed through her words. "Have you heard the news?"

"What news?" I'd had more than enough news for one day. I really didn't want any more.

"That wasn't Mr. Maranville's body you guys found. The sheriff's office confirmed it last night after somebody at the Post Standard found out and bugged 'em about it."

"What?"

"Duh. Watch my lips here, El. The body you found wasn't Mr. Maranville."

I stalled, trying to decide how much to tell Josie. "The face was burned but I don't understand how Diane could have made a mistake like that."

"She goofed, screwed up. Teachers do that sometimes, you know, even if everyone likes to pretend they don't."

Once again I was surprised to find Josie's reaction shaded so differently from my own. Teenagers inhabited a far different world, no doubt about that.

I decided to go with the truth, just not the whole truth. "Listen, I know the body wasn't Edward Maranville's. He came here last night. I thought he'd left, but this morning I found him on my porch, almost frozen to death. He's on the run from somebody."

I swore Josie to secrecy as I gave her the highlights of Edward's visit. I left out any mention of the gun or the missing painting. Keeping Diane Anderson's secrets was becoming increasingly difficult.

"El, you're some piece of work," Jose said with admiration -- at least I think it was admiration -- in her voice. "You can tell me more on our way."

"Our way?"

"We have to drive up to the Marlborough House right now. Billy Harris has got some info for you."

"Billy Harris?"

"Works at the inn. Built a fire for you guys that Sunday. Remember?

"What do you mean info?" I said.

"Something he's not supposed to tell. It's connected with Georgia O'Keeffe and it's way important. Bill's got the hots for me or I wouldn't have found out this much."

"Josie, you're talking crazy."

"Hey, you don't know what I went through to find this out for you -- a lot more than reading books and setting up interviews, I can tell ya."

"You didn't...?"

"Prostitute myself? Is that what you're asking, El? Close, but no banana, if you get my meaning." She let out a wild caw of laughter.

"My God," I said.

"Don't go all motherly-smotherly on me. I have to deal with enough of that from Kate. I do draw the line somewhere, you know."

I hardly dared think where that would be, but I felt myself weakening. A chat with Billy Harris over a late lunch had to be harmless, didn't it? "You probably wouldn't draw the line at lunch at the inn, would you?"

"Now you're talking, El."

A warning bell went off in my brain but I didn't pay much attention to it. I heard it, but I didn't – if you know what I mean. Like I was back on a New York street walking past a car with a shrieking theft alarm. Nothing that concerned me. I'd asked Josie for help with my O'Keeffe research, hadn't I? So she was helping me.

On the drive to the Marlborough House, she released a few more details. "I think Bill's found something that actually belonged to Georgia O'Keeffe. You're the big expert on her now. What could it be?"

"If he found something, why would he keep it a secret? Why can't he just tell you what it is?" I sounded annoyed, but my heart was racing with excitement.

We ran through a list of items O'Keeffe might have left behind at the lake -- a trunk, household goods, photographs Stieglitz had taken of her, one of her famous black dresses -- but I had only one thing on my mind -- paintings. Original paintings by Georgia O'Keeffe, a dozen or more of them, taken from the Andersons' summer house and worth what? I'd read up on their current value after I found the Red Canna. O'Keeffe paintings sold for hundreds of thousands of dollars. Of course, I wouldn't be the one selling them -- they wouldn't belong to me -- but the inside scoop on their discovery had to be worth plenty. An unknown journalist bursting on the scene with this story would be guaranteed a ticket to fame and fortune.

"This stuff Billy's talking about is in storage somewhere, like maybe in the basement? Right?" As I turned down the drive to the inn, I was picturing the room where Jack Whittemore had set up shop the night of the murder. There were probably a half dozen storage rooms like that on the lower level.

Josie snapped her shoulder belt nervously. "Not the

basement. Bill said something about a secret room."

"A secret room? Gimme a break. You've been reading too many Nancy Drew books," I said. But, as I pulled my van into the empty parking lot, I had to admit that the Marlborough House with its hulking, gloomy facade and uneven rows of windows looked like a place of many secrets.

Secrets maybe, but not guests. Foliage season had ended and the autumn influx of leaf peepers was over. The Christmas and ski crowds were almost two months away. The entrance hall/lobby was deserted. Billy Harris, his appearance much improved by khakis, blue dress shirt and navy tie, was manning the registration desk.

"Bill thinks there's something of Georgia O'Keeffe's here you'd be interested in. Don't you, Bill?" Josie gave him a meaningful glance as we approached the desk.

The boy didn't answer. He stared at Josie with deer-caught-in-the-headlights shock. His ears turned bright red.

"Bill's afraid of getting into trouble, aren't you Bill? He can't let us in the room where the stuff is."

Billy continued to stare, making no attempt to speak.

"What did you say the room number was -- 451?" Josie persisted. "That was it, wasn't it, fourth floor, room 451, but you can't give us the key, can you?" Josie shifted her gaze past him to a row of keys hanging behind the desk.

Billy's Adam's apple bobbed up and down as if he might be trying to swallow it, but no sounds came out of his mouth.

"Billy wouldn't be able to give us that key, anyway, would you, Bill? But he could let us take a master like the ones the cleaning people use."

Josie fixed her eyes on me, then stared hard at the keys. A gold key with a large M on it hung by itself on the left-hand edge of the row within easy reach. Her message was very clear.

"Oh I almost forgot, Bill," she said, reaching out to pat his arm. "I brought you one of Kate's hot pastrami sandwiches. They're still your favorites, aren't they? Come on over 'ere, I'll get it out for you." She produced a crumpled bag that had been stuffed into her sweatshirt pocket and strolled casually to the end of the counter.

Billy followed her. Josie dug into another pocket for a napkin and a can of soda and set him up for lunch. She hadn't quite mastered her mother's catering style, but her client didn't seem to mind. He reached for a chunk of the sandwich and began wolfing it down.

Before I could delve too deeply into the pros and cons of what I was doing, I grabbed the M key from the board and rushed out of the room. The winding staircase off the lobby was dark and steep. My knee protested, but I made it to the fourth floor in record time and emerged into a hallway almost as dark as the stairs. The brass numbers on the doors were easy to read. Room 451 was halfway down the corridor.

As I unlocked the door and swung it open, I caught my breath in surprise. I'd entered not the storage area I was expecting but the living room of a suite, freshly painted, furnished with elegant couches and spectacular antiques -- a cherry highboy, a leather-topped desk, Chippendale chairs. On the far side of the room windows, graced by mullions and leaded glass, framed a magnificent view of the lake. I could see the Narrows, looking nothing like it did in John's aunt's renderings, and beyond the eastern shoreline, the mountains stacked one on top of the other in soft shades of blue and purple. Once in a while something happens that makes me really discontent with my lot in life. The room did it to me that day. What must it be like to be rich enough to afford a setting like this, the furnishings, the view, the whole enchilada?

But a room with a view wasn't what I'd come here

to see. In the corner near the windows, a door stood open, revealing an empty closet with another door in its far wall. I slipped inside, ducked under some hangers and pushed open the second door. The room I entered was dark; the air, piercing cold. A freestanding screen in front of the wide-open windows blocked most of the light. As my eyes adjusted to the gloom, I made out a large worktable and an assortment of easels. I saw that the room was full of paintings -- propped on the easels, leaning against the walls -- shadowy, indistinct forms in the half-dark.

I fumbled for a switch and suddenly the room blazed with light. I didn't know where to look first. I'd gone through the looking glass into an enchanted garden, a garden full of gigantic flowers, lush and vivid, overwhelming in their color and beauty.

Here was Georgia O'Keeffe's flower life spread out before me in a dazzling tableau. I saw her petunias, glistening white with their sharp, pointy stamens, the velvety pansies, the amazing black iris, another version of the red canna, a jack-in-the-pulpit. I was staring at a visual feast -- I couldn't take it all in fast enough.

I moved slowly from one painting to another, identifying as many as I could. I was a million miles away when I heard someone in the closet. With my heartbeat clanging in my ears, I whirled around and knocked against one of the easels. As I reached out to steady the painting I'd almost sent flying, Josie came through the closet door.

"Thank God, it's you," I said.

She stopped short just inside the door. "Wow. Awesome."

"Awesome is right. I can't believe my eyes."

Josie followed my lead, going from one painting to another, commenting on those she recognized. She paused in front of the oriental poppies, now safely back on their easel. She squinted at their red-orange petals as if she was staring into the sun. "Isn't that the one they made the stamp of? She sure liked her flowers big," she said.

"She said she made them big so people would have to look at them, so they'd be startled by them," I told her.

O'Keeffe was right about that: I was startled by them. But she was wrong about something else. No matter what she claimed, there was sexual magnetism here beneath the forms. The room was charged with it. Maybe she hadn't acknowledged it, but what she'd created in these paintings was erotic, sensual, a landscape of hidden depths leading to a sensuous core.

"This really is a secret room, isn't it?" Josie said.

For the first time I looked at the room itself. She was right. There was no other door than the one from the closet, no other entrance, no exit to the corridor.

She shook my arm. "Come on, El. Now you've seen it, we've got to get out of here. I promised Billy you'd only need a minute."

I tried to take stock as she pulled me back toward the closet. The room had no furnishings except the worktable. Paintings stood everywhere, some in simple wood frames, others on canvas stretched over board or masonite. In a far corner I saw what I thought was a stack of watercolors. The one on top looked like the lake view I'd removed from Diane's frame. "Wait. Give me one more minute."

I'd started toward the watercolors when Billy Harris emerged from the closet.

"Is the guy coming?" Josie asked, her voice quavery.

Billy nodded, motioning frantically for us to hurry. He looked as if he were going to be sick.

"Is he on his way up right now?" Josie's fingers gripped my arm like a vise.

The boy nodded again, even more emphatically.

We pushed through the closet. Billy shut the inner door and reached out to rearrange the hangers. They swung and clinked together. One slipped from the rod and tumbled to the floor. I bent to retrieve it.

Billy shook his head and pushed me ahead of him. He reached for the key in my hand as he followed us into the hall. He had just turned the key in the outer door when we heard the groan of the elevator and the clatter of its door sliding open. Footsteps came toward us.

We started down the corridor, walking fast, not daring to look back.

The footsteps drew closer, then stopped before the door of the room we'd just left.

Billy stayed close behind us, hiding us as best he could. He pushed open the door to the stairs.

"Basement?" Josie asked him.

He nodded and picked up a tray of dirty dishes lying on the floor outside one of the rooms.

Josie and I ducked into the stairwell and flung ourselves down the steps. I still didn't dare look back, even when I thought I heard the door to the stairs opening behind us.

EIGHTEEN

We pounded down the stairs, desperate to get away as fast as we could. I kept listening for the man whose room we'd invaded to open the stairway door and charge after us, demanding to know what we'd been doing there. I felt as if the stairs went on forever. They finally ended in a basement corridor near a heavy steel fire door leading outside. Josie glanced toward the door and veered off in the opposite direction down a narrow hallway.

"Here. Can't we go out here?" I gasped.

Josie kept moving.

I realized we must be somewhere near the bar but I did a double take when Tom Durocher swaggered out of a door a few yards away. Josie and I both stopped dead in our tracks and stared at him as if he were the interloper instead of us. Tom swung around, as startled as we were. When he recognized us, his self-satisfied expression vanished, replaced by one of the guiltiest looks this side of B movies.

"What the hell are you two doing here?" He

reached back to yank the door closed behind him. I thought I heard a little murmur of surprise as he slammed it shut.

"Tom," I said.

"You trying to give me a heart attack? How did you get in here? Is Diane with you?" he demanded.

When someone bombards you with a series of questions, the last one, I've discovered, is often the most important. "No, Diane's not with us, but she is back from her trip." I watched for his reaction. For all I knew, he'd been with her over the weekend. Her visits to her son could be nothing more than a cover-up story for trips with Tom.

"The bar's not open yet so I can't invite you in for a drink. What are you doing here anyway?" Tom was trying hard but he couldn't hide his discomfort. There were sounds of movement inside the room he'd just left, but he pretended not to hear them.

Josie looked back over her shoulder toward the outside door we'd passed. "We came in the wrong way, I guess. Picking up some brochures for my mother's place. She likes to have 'em around when tourists ask about places to stay."

Tom didn't quite buy her explanation but he wanted us out of there bad enough not to question her further. The rustlings inside the room were growing louder.

"Go back through that door and take the outside steps to the terrace. You can get to the lobby that way. Here, I'll walk you down and show you."

He shepherded us quickly along the hall, but not so quickly I didn't see the slow turn of the doorknob as we started away.

"Hey -- what do you think Tom Terrific was up to?" Josie asked as soon as we reached the van. Excitement transformed her. Her dark eyes sparkled; her cheeks glowed with color.

"What's your take on it?" I tossed the question back to her. My head was full of the flower paintings. I didn't much care what Tom was doing unless it was somehow connected to them.

"He was hiding somebody, that's for sure, somebody he doesn't want Diane to know about."

"You think?"

"El, get with the program. He was doin' something in that room he didn't want us to know about."

"Maybe he brings his dog to work and has to hide it in there," I teased, playing devil's advocate.

She snorted. "Oh sure. A dog that turns doorknobs. Get real. This is serious stuff. He had a make-out session goin' in there and he's freaked we'll tell Diane."

I conceded the point. "Just kidding about the dog. But forget Tom for now. Let's brainstorm about the paintings. I want to be sure we both saw the same things in that room."

"Good. We're in business then," Josie said.

"Business?"

"The crime solving business."

"We're doing research here, nothing more."

Josie nodded agreeably. "Gotcha. Have it your way. I'll start. Billy told me you'd want to see what was in that room. I was right about that, wasn't I?"

"Yes, you were. I didn't get a chance to count the paintings, but I'd estimate twelve to fifteen."

"Yeah. Oil paintings. I know oils from my art class. All flowers. Right again?" she said.

"Right again. And those paintings sure looked like Georgia O'Keeffe's work to me. I think they're the missing paintings everybody talks about."

"But I didn't see her name on any of them. They weren't signed, were they?"

"She didn't sign her paintings, just put OK on the back sometimes. When I first started my research, I checked on that."

"You sure about that, El? I thought all artists signed

their stuff."

"She didn't. She was asked about that once and she said, 'you don't sign your face, do you?'"

Josie pursed her lips -- definitely in admiration this time. "She must have been one tough broad. I wish I'd known her."

"Me too. So we agree they were all oil paintings except for that stack over in the corner. Those looked like watercolors to me and the top one was a view of the lake. Maybe the others were too. Those could be watercolors someone fits into the frames to hide the O'Keeffe oils," I said.

"Why the heck would anyone do that?"

"Because O'Keeffe paintings are worth mega bucks."

"But why hide them?"

I liked bouncing ideas back and forth with Josie. "Let's go back and take this one step at a time. Old, supposedly worthless watercolors of the lake were stored for years in the Andersons' summerhouse. Then, all of a sudden they weren't there any more."

"Yeah, I heard Diane had stuff stolen. That's what it was -- paintings of the lake?'

"Yes, paintings she'd never liked, always wanted to get rid of. John insisted they couldn't dispose of them. He even built a special closet for them. Almost sounds like he knew they were valuable."

Josie shrugged. "If he knew that, why would he sit on 'em all those years? Why didn't he sell 'em? Unless that's what he's doing now."

"You mean he might have already sold them to someone over at the inn?"

"I doubt it. They'd be crated up or something if they'd been sold, wouldn't they? More like somebody's trying to sell 'em. The inn's owners could be letting him have a sale or an auction maybe. They do that in motels around here sometimes."

"Really?" I said.

"Yeah. I've seen ads in the newspaper for art auctions in motels. A friend of mine and I even saw one going on last year. People were shooting their hands up like crazy and the stuff was really dumb looking, nothing like these paintings."

"You may be onto something. You're good at this brainstorming stuff. Did Billy say who rents that suite?" I asked.

"I don't think he knows any of the guests' names. He doesn't usually work the desk."

"I keep thinking about that man Louise and I talked about -- Ted Reid. He hung onto O'Keeffe watercolors all his life. She gave them to him when he was in college and he wrapped them in brown paper and stored them away. Never told anyone he had them, even his family."

"Why not? Didn't he know she got famous."

"Maybe not at first, but eventually he must have. I guess he had his own reasons. So maybe John Anderson's been hanging on to them for his own reasons too."

Josie shook her head and gave me an exasperated look. "El, that doesn't explain anything. You gotta come up with something better than that."

"I don't know why he kept them so long. Unless he just found out recently they were the lost paintings. Diane told me he has a cousin in New Mexico who thought she was entitled to half of them. Maybe he didn't want her to know about them," I said.

"Didn't want to share the wealth, huh?"

"If the paintings are genuine O'Keeffe oils, they must be incredibly valuable, but I don't know how many people would have a claim to them -- John and Diane, the cousin, the O'Keeffe estate, who? Even Edward Maranville seems to think he owns at least one of them. But it sure looks like somebody took them from Diane's closet and moved them to the inn."

Josie stopped me. "Hey, hold on a minute. I'm supposed to disagree with you when I want to. Right?"

"Right. That's part of what makes it brainstorming."

"I wish you'd introduce this idea to my mother. How come you're so sure the paintings at the inn came from the Anderson place?"

Another good question. It was time to tell Josie the whole truth. "Well, coincidence is a big factor here, but it's an important one. The Andersons are missing a dozen or so paintings. I'm not supposed to tell anybody but there was one left in the closet and Diane brought it to me to hide for her. I took it apart and found an O'Keeffe flower painting like the ones we just saw hidden behind the watercolor. Then somebody stole it from me."

"No way. And you didn't tell me. Some partner in crime you are."

"I know. Diane swore me to secrecy, but I'm telling you now. So figure this. We've just found other O'Keeffe flower paintings like the one Diane brought to me. And didn't that look like a stack of watercolors in the corner? If I took a painting apart and found an O'Keeffe underneath, couldn't anybody else have done the same thing?"

"I still say you can't be sure the paintings we saw today came from Diane's place. Maybe other people have them too," she insisted.

"Well, I admit the Red Canna wasn't there. That's the one Diane brought for me to hide. So whoever stole it from me didn't take it to the inn. At least they haven't taken it there yet."

"Maybe they put it back where it came from," Josie said.

I was only half listening. Suppose Josie was right. Suppose the paintings hadn't come from the Andersons' after all. "Too bad we didn't see the back of any of the paintings. That's where the provenance is. Maybe that would have given us some clues."

"Don't go hoitytoity on me, El. What the hell is a provenance?"

"Sort of a history of a painting, where it's been hung, what galleries and shows it's been in."

"You mean we've got to go back to the inn and look for that?"

"Absolutely not. What we did wasn't right, Josie. You know that. I should never have taken that key and gone in that room," I said.

"But you did. That's why I like you."

Josie meant her words as a compliment, but I didn't take them that way. Here I'd insisted we couldn't play detective and that's exactly what we'd been doing. And we'd almost got caught breaking into somebody's room. In spite of my promises to myself, I'd put us both at risk. I had a lot of thinking to do about my relationship with this girl.

But not quite yet. As we approached the northern outskirts of Lake George Village, I tried once more to get a handle on what we'd seen. "Listen, Josie. Let's go back in time. Somebody -- John Anderson or anybody else for that matter -- finds paintings he thinks are the work of Georgia O'Keeffe. So then what would happen?"

"You're asking me? How do I know? I guess first of all he'd try to make sure if she really did paint them."

I thought of Edward's conversation with Martin Cascadden, the O'Keeffe expert.. "And then..."

"If the person was honest, he'd call a museum or an art gallery and find out what to do. If he was a crook, he'd try to sell 'em under the table."

"That's about what I'd say too," I said as we pulled up in front of Josie's house.

Before I could comment further, Kate flung open the front door and marched down the sidewalk toward us. She must have been watching for Josie.

"Oh, oh. Trouble. I'm supposed to be grounded." Josie took her time getting out of the van.

"Damn it, Josie," I heard Kate say. She kept her voice too low for me to hear the rest of her words, but I could tell she was angry. In fact, she was more than angry; she was furious -- and she didn't even know where we'd been or what we'd done.

I got out and walked around the van toward them. "Kate, I'm sorry. I didn't realize."

"Of course, you didn't. You see a totally different person than I do. You have no idea what really goes on around here."

I'd never seen Kate so upset. And her anger was directed not just at Josie but at me. I thought of myself as her friend and here I was, adding to her problems with her daughter. "Kate, I'm sorry. I'm in the wrong here, I know it. I haven't been thinking clearly. Please forgive me."

Kate shook her head. Did she mean she couldn't forgive me? I felt as if I'd taken a punch in the pit of my stomach. This was like having my grandmother mad at me. That hadn't happened very often but when it did, I wanted to curl up and die. "Kate..."

She waved her hand in a dismissive gesture and turned to go back to the house. Josie gave me an unreadable look and followed. Neither of them looked at me as I climbed into my van and drove away.

NINETEEN

I drove home in a funk, almost veering into a dark blue car that whizzed by me on Cove Road. Get a grip, I told myself, everything will fall into place sooner or later. But, as I unlocked the door to my uncle's camp, I wasn't thinking about Georgia O'Keeffe and the mystery cache of paintings I'd seen that afternoon. I was consumed with thoughts of Kate. Her friendship was important to me and I'd hurt her, angered her, perhaps alienated her for good.

I threw my jacket on a chair in the living room and started a fire. No sense waiting for Kevin to come and do it. It was obvious now he wasn't going to be around when I needed him. Granted I'd assured him on the phone the night before I had everything under control but, if I'd said I wanted him to come over, what difference would that have made? His family came first; I was kidding myself if I thought otherwise.

The fire took hold quickly, blazing up fierce as my thoughts. I didn't need a man to build one for me, any more than I needed one to fix me a drink. I found an opened bottle of white wine in the refrigerator and filled one of Aunt Mattie's crystal wineglasses to the brim. The glasses were fragile and delicate, etched with a pretty, geometric border, but they were small, too small for my purposes. I'd buy some new ones the first chance I got. I wasn't going to drink out of jelly glasses the way my mother had eventually done. I was above that, at least.

I stared into the flames, willing myself to recall everything I'd seen at the inn that day, to transfer the details into my long-term memory bank before a single one escaped. Then I'd decide what conclusions I could come too. No more pious thoughts about leaving the detecting to Jack Whittemore. I was determined to figure out what was going on.

First on the agenda: the secret room. Why, I asked myself, would the Marlborough House have a room that didn't open onto the corridor, a room whose only entrance was through a closet? Hardly what you'd expect to find in a hotel or inn. Except, of course, the builders of the mansion hadn't intended it for paying guests; they'd built it as a private residence. Perhaps that part of the top floor had been a nursery or a two-room suite of some kind. I'd picked up a book at Crandall Library with information about the mansions on the lake, including the Marlborough House, but I'd left it in the van. I didn't relish the idea of walking through the dark yard to get it. I'd do that in the morning.

I switched on the computer. As I waited for the dial into my server, I closed my eyes and tried to reconstruct my experience that afternoon. I'd walked through a closet into a surreal world, luxuriant in its splendor. I'd entered a secret garden, seen flowers in a different way than I'd ever seen them before.

My search engines waited to do my bidding. Research had come a long way since my college days, when the Readers' Guide and the library's card catalog were the starting points. I'd already bookmarked several sites for Georgia O'Keeffe. The one where I'd found the Red Canna was particularly strong on her flower paintings. I clicked on it and sat sipping my wine as the tricolored symbols expanded and filled their little frames with miniature versions of some of the very paintings I'd seen that afternoon. A calla lily had been propped on one of the easels, a pair of velvety pansies on another, the orange-red Oriental poppies on a third. I grabbed a pen and began to list them -- petunias, autumn leaves, a jack-in-the-pulpit and an elongated red canna very different from the close-up of the canna Diane had brought me. O'Keeffe had done that version later, I saw as I checked the dates, zooming in and cropping the flower the way Stieglitz cropped his photographs to reveal what she called her subject's core essence.

So what did it all mean? If the paintings were depicted in books and on the Web, they were already out there in galleries and museums somewhere. They hadn't been hidden away in Lake George from the time she painted them. And they couldn't all have been stolen and brought here. That would have been impossible, but...

O'Keeffe, I knew from my reading, had often done several versions of her flower paintings, destroying the ones she wasn't satisfied with. Louise had mentioned a story about a Stieglitz housekeeper who, instead of burning paintings as she'd been told to do, had given them to a neighbor to keep for her. Could that neighbor have been John's aunt? She'd lived near the Stieglitz property, hadn't she? She could have been the housekeeper's friend easily enough. No matter what Josie said, I was convinced the paintings at the inn were the paintings taken from Diane's closet.

I clicked onto another O'Keeffe site. While I waited for a response, I went to the kitchen to refill my wineglass. As I leaned into the open refrigerator and reached for the wine, a rush of memory catapulted me back to the evening before. I'd been standing in exactly the same way when I spun around to find Edward Maranville holding a gun on me. I'd been more frightened last night than I cared to admit. I'd thought he was going to kill me, but I'd gotten the better of him. So, why was I running scared now, putting off going to the van for a book I needed? If I wanted that book, I didn't have to wait until morning. I'd simply go get it.

I grabbed my car keys and the biggest flashlight I could find and slipped into Ray's heavy coat. The smell of raw wood and cooking odors and kerosene reminded me so powerfully of my uncle and the past that I felt tears prick at my eyes. A blast of bitter cold air slammed into me as I hurried through the little entryway between the kitchen and the back door. I moved quickly up the slate sidewalk, shivering with the cold, beaming the flashlight ahead of me. I reached the van and dug deep into the pocket where I'd put the keys. My fingers traced the edges of a large hole. The keys were gone.

I scuffed slowly back toward the camp, playing the light along the leaf-covered walk. The dry leaves made loud crackling noises in the silence. Why hadn't I waited until morning? Even Ray's heavy coat was no match for the piercing wind. I pulled up the hood and huddled deeper inside the coat, bent almost double to the ground, my face stinging from the cold. I stepped carefully along, setting my feet down gingerly, fearful that an accidental kick could send the keys flying.

Suddenly, strong arms wrapped around me from behind, pinning my own arms to my sides. I was held in a powerful grip, unable to pull away. The flashlight fell to the ground. I kicked back as hard as I could. My foot connected with a heavy boot but the grip didn't loosen. I tried to pitch myself forward, hoping to pull my attacker off balance, but his feet were planted firmly on the ground behind me and I couldn't budge him. I kicked back again; he grunted in pain as I hit his shin but he didn't loosen his hold.

"Let me go," I cried.

"Ellen?" The arms fell away. It was Kevin's voice. "I thought you were a prowler. What the hell are you doing out here?"

I twisted away from him, relieved and angry in equal measure. "Kevin, you almost scared me to death. Things are getting too much for me around here. Mugged in my own yard."

He leaned down to rub his instep. "I didn't exactly mug you. I'm probably the more seriously injured party here, if the truth were known. What in the world are you looking for? And where did you get that coat?"

"Help me find my keys and I'll explain." I picked up the flashlight

Surprisingly, Kevin held back on his questions as he scuffed along beside me. A few minutes later I saw the glitter of metal in the light of the flash. My keys. I hurried to the van and got the book.

"That's it?" Kevin asked.

"That's it. Let's get out of this cold," I said.

We stood shivering in the kitchen as I explained how Edward had been hiding in the camp the night before, how he'd waved a gun at me and demanded the painting.

"This was after you hung up on me?" Kevin's words flew at me with sharp, little barbs on them.

"I didn't hang up on you. I told you everything was all right and at that point it was."

"I heard today Diane made a mistake when she identified the body, that it wasn't Edward after all. Nobody seems to know where he is. Are you telling me he came here and threatened you with a gun and you didn't call the sheriff?"

"He was too nervous to be much of a threat. He wanted the Red Canna, claimed it belonged to him, but somebody had beaten him to it. I got the gun away from him and threw him out. He promised he'd work things out with Diane and then go to the sheriff himself. That was good enough for me." I heard the sharp, defensive edge that had crept into my voice. It wasn't an attractive sound.

"I'm trying to understand. Edward Maranville came here looking for the painting and he had a gun?" Kevin said again.

"That's what I'm telling you." I was even angrier now that my explanation had sounded so weak. I scrapped any idea of telling Kevin how I'd found Edward on the porch that morning and given him breakfast.

"I don't believe this, Ellen," he said. "I was hoping you wouldn't get yourself involved in this."

"And just what am I allowed to get involved in? Would you mind telling me that?"

He recoiled as if I'd hit him. We were still standing in the kitchen. He hadn't taken off his jacket and I hadn't ask him to. I'd kept my coat on too. I wanted him to leave. His remark had dredged up a lot of feelings I hadn't acknowledged even to myself. I felt like Susan Hayward in Back Street. Was that how he saw me too, as a kind of comfort woman, tucked away out of sight, good for sex and an occasional meal as long as I didn't get involved in anything else?

"Ellen, look. If you're mad because I couldn't get over here last night, I'm sorry. There was no way I could manage it," he said in a conciliatory tone. He glanced over my shoulder toward the fireplace. He knew I'd built the fire to prove I didn't need him, and he was smart enough to not to comment.

I didn't like having my mind read. "So, you couldn't come over. No problem."

"You did tell me everything was fine. If you're mad, say so. Let's talk about this."

"Not now. It's late and I'm tired. I've got work started I'd like to keep going with." I was driving the wedge deeper between us, but I didn't care. I was hurt, although I wasn't quite sure why. I wanted to hurt him too. Self-destruction can be very satisfying to me sometimes. I'm not my mother's daughter for nothing.

He started to protest, then changed his mind. "Okay. I'll go along then if that's what you want. Find a good hiding place for that gun tonight and turn it into the sheriff's department tomorrow." As always, the voice of reason.

"Right." I pictured Jack Whittemore's face if I took that piece of advice.

Kevin hesitated at the door. "Ellen...," he started.

I didn't give him a chance to say more. Some people can be just too damn reasonable. I pushed the door toward him. "Look, I really am tired. It hasn't been a great day."

He leaned forward as if to kiss me. I stiffened and pulled back. It was an involuntary move, really it was, but his eyes darkened as he realized what I'd done. He pushed his glasses up on his nose and gave me one of those long, penetrating looks guaranteed to make my knees go weak. I turned away fast before I could change my mind.

I waited until I heard his car pull away before I sat back down at the computer. I had to concentrate, to make a list of the paintings I'd seen at the Marlborough House. As long as I was guilty of breaking and entering—although I didn't know if it could be called that since I'd used a key—I might as well be clear about what I'd seen. Once I'd compiled a list of the paintings, then I'd speculate on where they'd come from.

I didn't want to think about any of the people I'd seen that day. I refused to spend one second recalling Tom Durocher's shenanigans or deciding why I was so suddenly and thoroughly out of sorts with Kevin. I wasn't small-minded enough to blame him for being a responsible father, was I? Something else must have ticked me off. I just wasn't sure what. And I certainly wasn't going to think about Kate and Josie. Any thoughts of them would be much too painful.

TWENTY

At eight o'clock the next morning I jumped out of the shower and pulled my best black wool suit from my New York days out of the closet. The suit, which had cost many, many lunches, transformed me into someone to be reckoned with -- at least I liked to think it did. I had no more time to waste. I was determined to find out what was going on.

The night before had left me reeling. I'd searched as many Web sites as I could, then switched off the computer and gone to bed. But, even with my eyes smarting with fatigue, I couldn't sleep.

The mess I'd made of things was mind-boggling. I'd not only worsened the rift between Josie and her mother but, by taking that key, I'd dug myself into a hole I didn't know how to climb out of. Maybe I should have listened to Kevin after all.

Someone should be told about the paintings, but who? If I went to Jack Whittemore and reported what I'd seen at the Marlborough House, I'd be in serious trouble. So would Billy and maybe Josie as well. Stealing a key and entering a guest's private suite was criminal trespass, wasn't it? I might not know the exact terminology for my offense but I suspected I could end up in jail and get Billy fired for his part in the hare-brained scheme. No way would confiding this piece of information to Jack Whittemore be a smart move.

I cast around for another solution. If the paintings had been taken from the Anderson cottage, as I suspected, wasn't it up to Diane and John to knock off their petty bickering and decide what to do about them? And shouldn't they want to make the decision together since the paintings, if they were authentic, could make them both rich? But the idea of trusting Diane to make a sensible decision in her current emotional state scared me to death. I couldn't predict how she'd react and I'd lost all my confidence in her good judgment.

Kevin, the one person whose judgment I did trust, was not available for comment. If he wasn't always so quick to bug me about getting involved, I could have told him about the paintings and let him introduce some badly needed common sense into the mix. But, it was too late for that now.

By the time I fell asleep at four o'clock, I'd pounded my pillow into submission a half dozen times, cut myself some slack and decided on a course of action. First, as soon as possible, I'd go to Kate -- on my knees if necessary -- and try to get back in her good graces. I'd take an oath never to let Josie talk me into anything again. That girl was a reincarnation of my own adolescent self and I knew from experience just how much havoc that troublesome little poltergeist could wreak.

Then, for the time being at least, I'd cool my jets with Kevin until I figured out exactly why I was so ticked off with him. As I tossed from one side of the bed to the other, I'd conceded that I couldn't fault him for urging me to butt out of an ongoing murder investigation. I should have reported seeing Edward to the sheriff's department, I had to admit that. And I didn't really blame him for staying home with a sick child, did I? I ought to be able to handle the fact that his life was full while mine was painfully empty. But, for that matter, so should he. We were as silly as Diane and Tom, trying to keep our relationship under wraps when everybody probably knew about it anyway.

As for my feature article -- I'd been spinning my wheels long enough. It was time to head in a new direction. Diane wasn't the only one with first-hand knowledge of the paintings stored at her summerhouse. John Anderson was co-owner of the cottage and its contents and I'd been pussy footing around, hesitant to seek him out. Edward had urged Diane to question John about the paintings. There was no reason I couldn't ask him some tough questions myself, get his take on what was going on. If I could find out how a collection of Georgia O'Keeffe flower paintings ended up tucked away in a private suite at the Marlborough House Inn, I'd have a world class hook for my article.

Anderson, Lowell Accounting occupied two floors of an attractive brick building on the main street of downtown Glens Falls. The exterior, newly sandblasted to a warm rose color, sparkled in the fall sunlight. The waiting area, with its thick carpets and overstuffed chairs, promised clients relief from their tax worries, at least until their accountant finished running their numbers.

The receptionist, a colorless little person ensconced behind a high mahogany counter, expressed grave doubts that Mr. Anderson would see me without an appointment. She shook her head sorrowfully. I nodded mine, empathized and persisted in my request. Eventually, she crumbled before my New York City assertiveness and agreed to ask him. She disappeared into an inner office and returned with good news. Mr. Anderson could spare me a few minutes. If I would follow her to the conference room...

John Anderson entered the small, rectangular meeting room from one door just as the receptionist ushered me in through the other. The conference room, despite its richly paneled walls and elegant table and chairs, boasted no distinguishing characteristics. Bland and lacking personality, it could have served any kind of business. The receptionist, equally bland, scuttled off as quietly as a little brown mouse.

John Anderson shook my hand in his firm CPA grip and motioned me to a chair at the massive table, which filled most of the room. He projected an image of importance but it was an image he'd bought and paid for -- tailor-made suit, Egyptian cotton shirt, a power tie that shrieked money and class, even an expensive after-shave. He conveyed no welcome, only a mild curiosity as to why I'd come. "I'm afraid I can give you only a few minutes this morning. I have a meeting starting and it is essential that I be on time for it. What can I do for you?"

I stiffened my spine and tried to appear half as confident as he did. "I'm writing a feature article on Georgia O'Keeffe and her years at Lake George. I understand your aunt was a neighbor of the Stieglitz family so I'm hoping you'll be willing to share some of her recollections of O'Keeffe with me."

The curiosity shifted to annoyance. "Really? That's why you've come? I assumed you were here out of concern for Diane. I remember meeting you at her condo the other day." The implication was clear. He was sorry he'd agreed to see me.

"I am concerned about Diane," I said quickly. "She's seemed quite distraught since we found the body and I must say I don't blame her. It was a distressing experience for both of us. I think the sooner she can put all this behind her, the better."

"Of course, but she's the only one who can do that."

I couldn't afford to waste the few minutes he'd offered me. I jumped in with both feet. "It might help her if we could clear up some of the questions surrounding the murder. Do you know who the murder victim was?"

He uttered an annoyed snort. "If I did, Ms. Davies, don't you think I would have told the sheriff's department?"

"For all I know, you have told them and they haven't released the name." I could see he was losing patience, but I plunged on. "What about the paintings that are missing from your cottage? Do you have any idea who took them or where they might be now?"

His expression didn't change but something happened behind his eyes. I'd trespassed into forbidden territory. "You should get Diane to share some of my aunt's comments on Georgia O'Keeffe with you. She always got such a kick out of them."

His effort to distract me worked for a minute. "You're saying that Diane knew your aunt? I hadn't realized that."

"Of course. That part of the lake was like a small community."

"So you both must have heard the rumors that O'Keeffe left paintings behind?"

"Property owners around there love those stories. Many attics have been cleaned out because of them." He twitched the corners of his mouth into a fake smile.

I countered with an equally phony smile. "But could there be a connection between those rumors and your missing paintings?"

"I don't see how, Ms. Davies, and I really don't have time for this now. If you'll excuse me..." He started to get up.

"Wait, Mr. Anderson. I must ask this. Is there a chance your missing paintings were done by Georgia O'Keeffe?"

He transformed the fake smile into a smug grin.

"Hardly. If you saw them, you would know what you're suggesting is outside the realm of possibility."

"I did see one of them. Diane assured me the others were very much like it."

"Then I don't understand why you've come to me with these ridiculous questions." He was on his feet now, scowling at me.

"But what do you think could have happened to the paintings in your closet?" Should I tell him straight out what I'd seen hidden behind the watercolor?

He didn't give me a chance to decide. "Listen here, Ms. Davies," he barked, "whether you realize it or not, you're contributing to a serious problem. In the last two years Diane has fought me on every issue -- money, the sale of our house, the disposition of our lake property, even whether or not our son should attend private school. Now she's gone off the deep end over some worthless paintings."

I stood up too and faced him across the table. "Mr. Anderson, I have reason to believe at least one of those paintings is the work of Georgia O'Keeffe."

A bright band of red appeared across his nose and cheeks. The lines around his mouth deepened; his eyes narrowed. He sucked in a long, ragged breath, clenching his teeth as if trying to steady himself. The conference room door burst open.

The receptionist poked her head through the opening. "Mr. Anderson, I'm so sorry. He won't wait. He insists on seeing you right now."

From the interior corridor came the sound of raised voices: one, high-pitched, fluttery, spewing out ineffectual protests; the other, a man's voice, slightly accented, thick and guttural, overlaid with anger, the voice I'd heard ordering Scotch at the Marlborough House the day we found the body.

"All right, Sydney. It's all right." Everything about John Anderson's tone and manner proclaimed his words a lie.

The receptionist clung to the door as if trying to block the opening. I could not see the man behind her, but I could hear him rumbling angrily.

"Tell Isabelle to show him into my office and say I'll be right there."

As the receptionist sidled away, John Anderson turned to me. "Ms. Davies, I told you I didn't have time for this. I hope you're satisfied. Now will you please leave before I have you evicted."

He whirled around and stormed out. His words erupted in a series of staccato bursts, bouncing back at me loud at first, then fainter as he moved away from me along an interior corridor. "Hold my calls, Isabelle. Cancel my appointments for the rest of the morning. I'll buzz when I want coffee brought in."

He was almost out of earshot when I heard his voice soften, his tone change to a warm, ingratiating purr. "Bertholdt, so good to see you again."

TWENTY-ONE

I braced myself against a lamp post in front of Anderson, Lowell Accounting, shaky as a drunk who'd been thrown out of a bar. I'd been escorted to the door, not by the timid young receptionist -- I could have taken her easy in hand-to-hand -- but by a large, rather burly associate in shirt sleeves who'd been summoned from his desk in the inner sanctum to hasten my departure.

"Don't put your hands on me. I'm leaving," I warned as he approached me. I'd tried for a snappier retort but that was the best I could do. I didn't exactly run for the door, but I was out of that office in a nanosecond. So much for my foray into the world of detecting. Josie would have been ashamed of me.

As soon as I'd composed myself, I sauntered down the street and ducked into a little eatery a few doors away. I needed a coffee break to steady my frazzled nerves and give me a chance to think. I'd stumbled onto something at the CPA office, I was sure of it, and John Anderson had been anxious to get me out of there before I figured out what it was. The man with the deep voice and the faint trace of an accent, the man John had called Bertholdt, had to be Edward's friend, Bertholdt, the man we'd seen at the inn. There couldn't be two of them, could there? And Bertholdt had arrived primed for a rip-snorting argument. John Anderson had turned pale when he heard that voice.

I'd curled up in a booth and finished my first cup of coffee before my brain kicked into gear and I made a second connection. Sydney. Could the mousy little receptionist have been John's fiancée, Sydney Vanderhoff? From what Diane had said, I'd assumed the Vanderhoff heiress would be drop-dead gorgeous and enjoying a life of wealth and privilege. But, there was no reason Sydney couldn't hold down a job like most of the rest of the world and no reason she'd be drop-dead gorgeous either. My detecting skills needed a thorough overhaul, no doubt about that.

I looked up to see the plump, smiley-faced waitress behind the counter watching me. She shifted from one foot to another, holding out the coffee carafe to indicate I should bring over my cup for a refill.

"Maybe you can help me," I said as I approached her. "I'm looking for a Sydney Something-or-other. I think she works in one of the offices near here."

"Sydney Vanderhoff? Works over at Anderson, Lowell?" the woman asked.

That was easy enough. I'd redeemed myself a little anyway. "The CPA office?"

"Yup. She's the receptionist. For now, that is. Gonna marry the boss."

"Really? A receptionist's dream come true," I said.

"Doesn't need the money. Only child. Father's got the big bucks," she confided.

I pushed a few more buttons and got the full scoop on Sydney and John.

"Yup, Mr. Anderson divorced his wife for her. The ex is a teacher, real glamorous looking. Dynamite figure. Real nice auburn hair." She patted her own hennaed locks.

"Diane? I know her."

"Keeps herself looking great, doesn't she? So he swaps her for a plain Jane."

"Go figure," I said.

"But a rich Jane. That's the key."

"Money talks." I could be really profound when I put my mind to it. I ambled back to my booth. The hands of the clock crept slowly past eleven. The waitress busied herself behind the counter. I hoped she was expecting a noon rush. Otherwise, the little restaurant was going under.

I was reviewing my encounter with John Anderson, trying to decide if I was overlooking something important, when Sydney Vanderhoff marched in the front door. I ducked my head, hoping she wouldn't notice me, but I needn't have worried. She was focused on something far more important than me. She muttered a question that sent the waitress hurrying into the kitchen. Sydney paced nervously back and forth in front of a glass case filled with baked goods.

"Sorry. It didn't come in," the waitress said from the doorway.

"What do you mean it didn't come in? You ordered it. Bob guaranteed it for today." The timid manner vanished. Before my eyes, Sydney transformed herself into an angry shrew.

"I guess I could look again," the woman said, obviously stalling. This time her visit to the kitchen lasted several minutes. Sydney tapped her manicured nails on the glass.

Finally the waitress returned. "Sorry. Bob shouldn't have guaranteed it. He knows how unpredictable that bakery is."

The explosion, when it came, rocked the walls. Sydney yelled, threatened, banged on the counter. Eventually, she simmered down enough to pick out an assortment of pastries. She snatched the box from the waitress and flounced out, still in a major huff.

"Whew," I said as the door banged shut.

The woman poured herself a cup of coffee. "Whew is right. Refill? On the house."

"Thanks. Does that happen often?" I brought my cup to the counter again.

"Often enough, but we prefer our customers don't witness scenes like that."

"So what was the big deal?"

"That's the Sydney you were asking about. They have some special client comes to Anderson, Lowell. Has to have a certain kind of coffeecake. Can you believe it?"

"Some days it's hard to know what to believe," I told her and went back to my booth.

At twelve o'clock I telephoned Louise Cascadden.

"I'm so glad you wanted to stop by," she said as she opened her door to me half an hour later. "You can join me for a little lunch."

I sat at the worn trestle table in Louise's kitchen while she stirred a pot of homemade vegetable soup already simmering on the stove and pulled a pan of freshly baked corn muffins from the oven. I'd planned to ask clever questions, elicit a lot of information without giving much away, but there was something about sitting in that old-fashioned kitchen with those wonderful aromas swirling around me that loosened my tongue. I swore Louise to secrecy and told her about the paintings Josie and I had seen at the Marlborough House.

She didn't act surprised. Maybe one of the advantages of reaching eighty is that you're not surprised about much of anything. She nodded as I spilled out the story.

"You say they were all paintings of flowers -- cannas, petunias, poppies? I wonder if these are the same paintings Mr. Maranville was referring to when he spoke to my husband," she said.

"They could be. I understand Mr. Maranville spent time at the inn. Did your husband tell you exactly what he said?"

"As I recall, he asked Martin about rumors O'Keeffe had left paintings behind at Lake George when she moved to New Mexico. Wouldn't say where the rumors had come from. Martin got the feeling he was keeping something back."

"Do you think your husband could have seen the paintings at the inn or heard about them?"

"If he did, he didn't tell me. Did you recognize the paintings you saw? Did they look like photographs of them you've seen in books?"

"Yes, in books and on the Internet. I can't swear they were exactly like the photographs I've seen but they were very similar."

"Well, as I'm sure you know from your research, O'Keeffe often painted a number of versions of the same flower. Started doing her enormous flowers in 1924, did a series of the iris, the canna. The calla lily was a big favorite of hers. She may have started with the callas. There were so many of them."

"Seeing them all together in that room was an amazing sight. The paintings were huge. I felt like an insect in a garden," I said.

"Yes, she zoomed in on her flowers and cropped out the background. She believed colors and shapes conveyed more than words. In fact, I understand they've used a quote to that effect on the new museum in Santa Fe."

The soup boiled over with a fierce, hissing sound. Louise pushed herself up from the table and shuffled to the stove. "It's good to be cooking for someone," she said as she returned with two bowls of soup and placed them on the rush mats in front of us. She moved the basket of muffins closer to me. I dug in. The food was delicious.

"Another possibility keeps popping into my mind."

Louise lifted a spoonful of soup to her mouth and stared off into space.

"What? Tell me," I wanted to yell, but I could see she couldn't be hurried.

"Catherine," she said finally. "O'Keeffe came from a large family, you know. Her sister, Catherine..."

"Yes?" I said.

Another long pause. "Well, perhaps..."

"Yes?" I was ready to burst.

"There's a story that Catherine began doing flower paintings herself, paintings very similar to her sister's."

"Really? Copying O'Keeffe's work, you mean?"

"Oh, I wouldn't say that. Remember young women at the time often studied drawing and painting. Flowers were considered a proper subject for them. Perhaps it was only natural that Catherine would pattern her work after an older sister's."

"Did Catherine do many paintings?"

"Yes, I believe she did. At one point she sent some from Wisconsin to a gallery in New York—the Delphic Studios, it was called—morning glories, other flowers. Her paintings were very similar to O'Keeffe's."

"Were those paintings displayed in New York?"

"I don't think so. I suspect O'Keeffe would have vetoed that idea very quickly. Apparently, she was enraged when she saw them, didn't communicate with Catherine for four years until Catherine finally stopped painting. Now, Ida—she was another sister—painted too, but in an entirely different style."

"I've read that Catherine visited here in Lake George. Could she have done some of those flower paintings while she was staying here?"

Louise shook her head, obviously distressed. "Oh, Ellen, I don't know. You're looking for explanations. I don't have them. I can only suggest possibilities."

"Louise, I'm sorry. I'm afraid I've upset you. I didn't mean to push so hard. I want to stay open-minded." I broke off a piece of my muffin and buttered it slowly.

Louise had started my mind racing, but she was right. I'd been grasping for quick, easy answers instead of exploring the many different possibilities.

"Did you see the backs of the paintings at all? Did you see a provenance, a marking of any kind?" she asked.

"Unfortunately no. We only got a quick look. We didn't see anything like that at all."

"You can find out a lot from a provenance. You know what I mean by that, don't you? It tells the origin of the painting and something of its history as well."

I nodded. I'd stressed the importance of the provenance to Josie. Maybe I shouldn't have. I didn't want her going back to the Marlborough House to check out the paintings again.

I reached out and touched Louise's hand. Her skin was translucent, as soft as Connor's. "Louise, think a minute. Did Edward tell your husband he'd actually seen the paintings or had he just heard rumors they existed?"

She patted my hand affectionately. "Ellen dear, I don't know. This is a very painful subject for me to talk about. If you want, I'll let you have Martin's notes. Perhaps as you go through them, you'll find answers to some of your questions."

I couldn't believe my good fortune. I wanted to shout with joy. Instead, I forced myself to sit quietly while Louise made the long, arduous journey into her bedroom. She came back with a battered cardboard file bulging with papers. Martin had obviously kept voluminous notes.

"Let me help you with that," I said, but she turned away from me, hugging the file even tighter. She eased it onto the kitchen table, then stood staring down at it, finding the strength to let it go.

On my way down the mountain, with the file wedged tightly on the floor behind the driver's seat, I thought again about Louise's gentle rebuke. She'd zeroed in on the problem. I was grasping at explanations, instead of considering possibilities. I'd assumed the paintings I'd seen at the Marlborough House were authentic Georgia O'Keeffe flower paintings, but there were other possibilities I hadn't thought of -- Catherine O'Keeffe for one. Catherine had done paintings similar to her older sister's. Perhaps, the paintings at the inn were hers. Maybe that was why they'd been abandoned. Or they could be Ida's. Louise had said Ida's style was different, but what if at some point she'd tried her hand at flowers too? And, if I was willing to concede that someone other than Georgia O'Keeffe had done the paintings at the inn, couldn't the artist have been anyone else, anyone at all?

O'Keeffe was a genius, an original, but her work, especially her work from this period of her life, wouldn't be hard to duplicate. Her flower paintings were characterized by strong, bold forms and brilliant colors; there were no backgrounds, no complicated details. Almost anyone with artistic ability could copy them -- not just one of her sisters.

And -- I kept expanding on these thoughts – what if the paintings hadn't been done seventy or more years ago when O'Keeffe was summering at the lake? What if they'd been painted only recently? I remembered the faint smell of paint in the suite at the Marlborough House. I'd assumed the living room had been newly decorated, but perhaps the smell had come from the canvases in the next room. Was that why the windows in that room had been left opened to the wind off the lake -- to blow away the odor of paint?

I didn't want to make the same mistake again, grasp at another hasty explanation, but a question had popped full-blown into my head and I couldn't dislodge it. What if someone was copying O'Keeffe's work right now, someone who'd already killed once, maybe twice, to keep from being found out?

TWENTY-TWO

By six o'clock that night I'd sorted Martin Cascadden's notes into a dozen overflowing piles and arranged and rearranged them in a variety of patterns on my living room table. Martin's jottings touched on every aspect of Georgia O'Keeffe's life and work. His handwriting was that of an Edwardian gentleman -- charmingly old-fashioned but distressingly hard to read. I was staring at the notes, considering what to do next, when Kevin arrived.

"What in the world...? You're hoping to make sense of all this?" he said as he surveyed the cluttered table. If his feelings had been hurt by my behavior the night before, he didn't let on.

I followed his lead, glad to be back on friendly terms -- at least temporarily. "Good question. Louise has let me borrow Martin Cascadden's notes. He was thorough, no doubt about that."

"Can I help?" Kevin pulled out a chair and sat down across from me. He'd changed from the clothes he wore to work into khakis and a blue Polo shirt. His dark hair shone, still slightly damp from the shower. A little cut at his jaw line testified to a hurried shave. He smelled of shampoo, a fresh lemony scent I found very appealing. My father's heavy colognes had usually meant a date with a woman other than my mother.

I pushed a pile of small scraps of paper across the table. "Look through these, will you? Thank God, Louise said I didn't have to keep this stuff in any particular order. See if you can find anything that pertains to O'Keeffe's summers at Lake George or to her flower paintings. That's all I'm looking for right now. Nothing about New Mexico or her later work."

Kevin pushed his glasses up on his nose, a sign of serious purpose. "Before I start, have you heard from Maranville since he left here? The sheriff's department wants to talk to him."

I didn't exactly lie. "Diane took him somewhere. They're going to call Jack Whittemore, at least they said they would." I had a perfect opening to tell Kevin about the paintings but I wasn't quite ready to confess my latest transgression to him.

We sat quietly for a time, intent on our decoding. Martin had written his notes on anything that fell under his hand -- used envelopes, half sheets of paper, index cards, even sunny yellow post-its. Many of the facts he'd recorded meant nothing when there was no way to tell the period in O'Keeffe's life they referred to. The pile we called miscellaneous kept growing until it looked like Mount Vesuvius ready to erupt.

Kevin's powers of concentration always impressed me. He hunkered down over the notes, studying, analyzing, squinting at the almost illegible words, wrinkling his forehead as he puzzled over them. His presence was distracting. As I watched him, I felt a familiar rush of warmth, the pleasant stirrings of physical desire. Just how annoyed with this guy was I anyway?

He finished sorting through the pile I'd handed him and looked at me for a long minute before he spoke.

"I'd like to take you out for something to eat. You haven't eaten already, have you?"

"No," I said.

"It's after seven."

"I know," I said.

"I told Cindy I was seeing you. I stopped by the house at lunch time and told her."

"How did that go?" I knew Kevin's ex-wife must have been upset by the news. Two years ago she'd initiated their divorce; recently she'd been pushing for a reconciliation.

"Not well. But I haven't felt very honest lately. It's going to be hard for her to let go, but she has to do it."

He'd taken a major step, I knew that, but I didn't let him off the hook. "Letting go is hard for everyone. I've had some tough experiences with that myself."

"So do you want to go out for something to eat?"

"We could probably get a pizza delivered," I heard myself saying. I couldn't believe I'd said it. He'd picked up on what was bothering me and he was doing something about it. Tonight's invitation wasn't just about going out to eat. He was changing the equation, moving our relationship to a different level and I was holding back, reluctant to go along. What did I want anyway? I wasn't trying to force a commitment. Louise must be right about my need to pin everything down. Why couldn't I leave myself open to possibilities the way he was doing?

We kicked the subject of dinner around like kids with a soccer ball. In the end we went out for a pizza. I couldn't decide if I'd compromised or capitulated. As we waited for our order, we talked about Martin's notes, staying away from anything more personal. I found myself thinking about Georgia O'Keeffe, about how little independent spirit she'd shown when she first came to Lake George. In those days she'd gone along with Stieglitz in almost everything -- spending summers at the lake when she wanted to travel, helping run the family home when she longed for privacy and time to paint. When Stieglitz's divorce was final, she'd married him even though she wasn't sold on the idea of marriage, given up thoughts of children because he'd insisted they shouldn't have them. When I considered her life as a whole, I found it hard to believe she'd ever been so acquiescent.

Kevin was deep in his own thoughts too. We left the restaurant as soon as we finished eating. Our presence failed to provoke a town scandal; no one paid any attention to us.

When we pulled into my uncle's driveway, he left the motor running. "You have work to do, I know. Should I come in?" he said.

It was my move. He was waiting for me to invite him in. Unconsciously, I parroted the words I'd used the night before. "Well, I do want to keep at those notes. Thanks for understanding."

"I'm not sure I do understand. But maybe when you get this article off your mind..."

What? I thought. I'd stop acting so impossible? I opened the car door and a blast of cold air hit me. "Wow, it's cold."

"Want me to come in and make a fire so you don't have to lose the time? I'd just get it going for you. I wouldn't have to stay."

"No need," I said, but I was touched. I pulled the door shut and turned back to him. "No, but thanks, thanks for everything, the pizza, the..." I leaned toward him and put my hands on his cheeks. They were as cold and smooth as the strip of ice frozen along the edge of the driveway. I kissed the place where the little twitch rippled in his jaw when he was upset, then I slid my lips across his face until I reached his mouth. An electrical charge slammed into me. I knew he felt it too because he pulled me tight against him and kissed me back until we were both gasping for breath. Then, like the big dope I was, I jumped out of the car and ran for the house.

I couldn't let myself think about Kevin right then. I had too many conflicting feelings to sort through. Figuring out what I wanted would take a lot longer than one evening. O'Keeffe might have been acquiescent in her early years here, but she'd asserted herself soon enough, turning a little shanty on the property into her own private work space, traveling alone on short visits to the Maine coast, later taking extended summer trips to New Mexico. And here I was, seventy-some years later, wondering if I could share my life with a controlling man without sacrificing my own identity. Women might have made progress in those years but the basic questions still had to be answered by each individual.

I sat down at the table and went back to work. At eleven o'clock I unfolded a pocket-sized piece of paper and knew I'd found what I was looking for -- a list of flower paintings, arranged not by date and not by the kind of flower portrayed. I closed my eyes and pictured the room at the Marlborough House. The paintings on Martin's list were the paintings I'd seen in that room. He'd included a couple I hadn't seen there -- the Red Canna was one of them -- but I thought I understood why. The Red Canna had been taken from the room and brought to the Anderson cottage some time after Martin had been there; perhaps the other painting had been removed too before I saw the room. This time I was determined to consider a range of possibilities, but I was sure of one thing: Martin Cascadden had been in the secret room and had seen most of the same paintings Josie and I had seen there.

If only he hadn't been killed so tragically. The warning buzzers in my head began beeping louder. Martin had visited that room, seen the paintings and a short time later he was dead. Edward had asked questions about the paintings and not long afterward, another man was dead, a man who looked enough like Edward for Diane to identify the body as his. Was Edward right in thinking the murderer had really meant to kill him? Was it because Edward, like Martin, had found out something he wasn't supposed to know?

I glanced toward the kitchen door. I'd locked up for the night when I came in but I hadn't slid the bolt across. I jumped up to do it. Not that it would matter much if someone wanted to get in, I'd found that out already. I shuddered. I too knew something I wasn't supposed to know and I wasn't the only one. Josie and Billy had seen what I saw. Had I put them at risk too, along with myself?

Two men were dead and more than a dozen paintings, quite possibly long lost works by America's most famous woman artist, were hidden away at the Marlborough House Inn. Were they the same paintings that had been taken from the Andersons' summerhouse? Had I been right in thinking they were the lost O'Keeffe paintings people at Lake George had speculated about for years, or were they only copies? And, if they were copies but people thought they were the real thing, wouldn't they still be incredibly valuable?

Other questions, equally perplexing, tumbled about in my head. Edward Maranville had insisted the Red Canna belonged to him and he'd threatened to kill me for it. What did he know that I didn't? And how did the Andersons fit into all this? I knew I was on John's blacklist but I'd thought Diane was my friend. I'd called her and left messages several times after I got home from Louise's and she hadn't returned my calls. Once again, I didn't know what to think about her.

As I searched for answers, I flipped the list over in my hand. A telephone number with a 212 area code was scrawled across the back. A New York number. Martin Cascadden had written a New York telephone number on the back of his list. It was after midnight but midnight wasn't all that late in the city. I'd had friends there who thought nothing of calling me at one or two in the morning. I punched out the number.

The phone rang four times. A curt, clipped voice on an answering machine said: “Okay, you’ve reached me. Leave your name and number after the beep and I’ll call you back.” That was it. No hint as to who it was.

“Name: Martin Cascadden,” I said and gave my own telephone number.

TWENTY-THREE

Josie Donohue had been missing for almost forty-eight hours before her mother called me.

"I didn't really think you'd let her stay at your place without telling me," Kate said, "but I had to be sure. I'm getting more worried by the minute. I just found out she wasn't in school yesterday or today."

I'd launched into my prepared apology when Kate cut me off.

"It's not your fault, Ellen, I've told you before. You see a totally different side of her than I do. The other day after you left we had a major blow-up because she'd gone off when she was supposed to be grounded and she stormed out. It's not the first time she's done that."

"Do you have any idea where she went?"

Kate tried to sound calm but her underlying worry clanged through loud and clear. "She has friends she can stay with but she wouldn't hang out at any of their houses all day. She'd go to school. Ordinarily, the attendance office calls and checks when a student's absent, but there was some kind of mix-up. By the time the secretary reached me, Josie had been out for two days. I don't like this at all."

You don't like it, I wanted to say, and you don't know the half of it. But I didn't see the point of scaring Kate even more. Josie pulled some weird stuff on her mother; maybe this latest escapade had nothing to do with our visit to the inn. "How can I help?"

"Just let me know if she turns up at your place. That's all you can do. Jake claimed he hadn't seen her and I got the feeling he was telling the truth. As soon as I hang up, I'm going to call some of her other friends. So far nobody admits knowing anything."

I stared out the window at the lake. It wasn't four o'clock yet but the horizon had disappeared. Water and sky flowed together, dark and ominous as my thoughts. Kate might be willing to let me off the hook, but I couldn't ease up on myself. I ran through my last conversation with Josie. We'd been driving back from the Marlborough House. Still stunned by what I'd seen there, I'd paid little attention to her chatter. We'd talked about the missing Red Canna. What was it Josie had said -- something about the thief putting it back where it came from? She'd meant the Anderson cottage, I suppose, and I hadn't considered that very likely. But she'd thought she was onto something, even suggested we drive back up there to look.

I tried to get inside Josie's head. If I could just drop a few years -- okay, drop a decade and a half -- and slip back into thinking the way I'd thought when I was a teenager, maybe I could come up with something. If Josie wanted to check out the Anderson cottage, she could manage it easily enough on her own. I'd mentioned the house key in the flower pot, even told her where the key to the closet was hidden. I'd made everything so easy for her. Josie didn't have a car, but getting a ride wouldn't be a problem for a gifted conniver like her. And then if she'd wanted a place to stay, why not hang there at Diane's for a while, show her mother she couldn't boss her. The more I thought about Josie pulling a trick like this, the more convinced I became I was on the right track.

But there was something else, something I couldn't quite get a hold of. Maybe if I stopped trying so hard, it would come to me. I decided to call Diane again. This time I'd ask her to ride up to the lake with me.

Once again, Diane didn't answer. I was left on my own.

I didn't feel a bit guilty fishing through the flower pot for the key to the Andersons' front door. Breaking and entering was second nature to me now. But Diane's cottage and the empty camps around it gave me the creeps. I felt as if I'd stumbled into a village of the damned. I almost expected scary music to start playing and the ghost of the murdered man to come wafting out of the living room toward me. If Josie had stayed here alone overnight, she was a lot braver than I was.

I switched on the hall light and dashed up the stairs and into the front bedroom for the key to the closet. No matter what Josie thought, I was sure the closet would be empty. Diane had removed the one painting left there and brought it to my house and I doubted that anyone had put it back. I slid the door open and dug deep into my shoulder bag for my little flashlight. When I turned it on, I couldn't stifle my startled cry. The sight that greeted me was the same sight I'd seen that afternoon with Diane -- one painting draped in a piece of sheeting, leaning against the back wall of the closet. Even those little tracks in the dust looked untouched. Josie had been right: whoever had stolen the painting had put it back where it came from.

I took hold of the frame and carried the painting, still covered by the sheet, into the bedroom. What should I do -- steal it back? After all, Diane had brought it to me. Or should I leave it here and tell her I'd found it? I turned on a lamp and pulled the sheet away.

The painting I was staring at wasn't the Red Canna. It wasn't an ugly lakescape or one of the paintings from the Marlborough House Inn. It was -- I recognized it -- the Black Iris III, one of O'Keeffe's several versions of the black iris, breathtakingly beautiful, its hues rich and dark and haunting. I'd read about it, seen it in books and on the Net, compared it to Stieglitz's nude photograph of O'Keeffe in which he seemed to be depicting the artist herself as the black iris. Here was the flower painting believed by many to be the most exquisite of them all. This time I looked quickly at the back for the provenance. There was nothing there. But the act of looking for it jogged my memory. That was second thing Josie had talked about on our ride home, wasn't it? She'd mentioned going back into that room at the Marlborough House to look for a provenance.

A ball of ice formed deep in my gut. She wouldn't be that crazy, would she? We'd almost been caught once. She wouldn't dare take that kind of chance again. The ice kept expanding, filling me with a sickening fear.

I put the painting back in the closet and locked the door carefully, taking pains to leave everything the way I'd found it. The walk from the front door to my van was torture. Someone had been murdered in this cottage. For all I knew, the murderer was still lurking nearby, watching me. I felt a tingle run down my back, as my spinal column stiffened, anticipating the knife. The ball of ice in my gut turned into a glacier.

The minute I got in the van I locked the doors and went tearing back up the road toward the shortcut to the Marlborough House. Billy Harris, be working today, I pleaded. Don't let this be your day off. He'd know if Josie had come back there. If I could only convince him to tell me.

Heavy, black storm clouds scudded low over the lake. The wind unleashed an ugly keening. The Marlborough House towered, majestic and forbidding above the swaying trees, a setting straight out of a Stephen King novel.

The inn's massive front door was locked. I banged the brass knocker over and over again, but there was no answer. I grabbed the wrought iron handle and tried to rattle the door in its casing. It didn't budge. Panicked, I started across the stone terrace to take the stairs down to the bar. Suddenly, I heard footsteps behind me. A bearded man in shabby work clothes materialized at my elbow.

The man leered at me, leaning in too close. "Nobody here now, Miss. They're closed."

"Closed? What do you mean, closed?"

"This time of year they close up for a while. No business. I 'spect they'll be open for Christmas. Come back then."

"The bar? Isn't the bar open?"

"Told ya, Miss. They're closed."

"When? When did they close?" I was shouting at him now over the wind.

"Yesterday. They closed the whole place down. Like every year."

"How can I get in touch with someone who works here? It's important. I've got to get in touch with him."

He smirked. At least four of his upper teeth were missing, the ones remaining were yellow and crooked. "Young Mr. Trev don't let me give out his phone number, Miss. We don't give out no information like that at all."

"I don't want... Never mind." I turned to go. I had to find a way to get in touch with Billy Harris. I had to know if Josie had been here.

TWENTY-FOUR

My search for Josie hadn't netted a single clue, but I wasn't about to give up. I headed back to my uncle's camp, determined to call all the Harrises in the telephone book until I found Billy or someone who knew how to reach him. I'd even call Tom Durocher if necessary, I thought; maybe he could help me. If I didn't connect with Billy or Tom, I'd call Kate back, tell her the whole story and urge her to report Josie's disappearance to the sheriff.

I tossed my jacket onto a chair, paying little attention to the streaks of dust down the front from Diane's closet or the red stain on the sleeve from my pizza with Kevin. I was reaching into the desk drawer for the phone book when I realized there was a message on my answering machine. I stopped short and pushed the play button.

The same gruff voice I'd heard the night before said, "Martin Cascadden, get in touch ASAP. I'll wait here for your call."

I dialed the New York number and started to explain who I was.

The man on the other end of the line cut me off, as brusque on the phone as he was on his machine. "Put Martin on."

"Martin's dead," I said. I could be pretty brusque myself.

"Dead? How?"

I'd startled him. I could hear surprise in his voice. Something more than surprise. I told him about the accident.

"Were the cops up there satisfied it was an accident?" he asked.

"Not sure. I found this number in his notes. Who are you anyway?"

He hesitated.

I let the question hang there. "I'm not telling you anything else until I know who you are."

"Okay. I'm a detective. Art crime specialty. Joe Grazzia's the name. It doesn't matter right now who I'm working for."

"And you deal with....?"

"The three F's -- frauds, fakes and forgeries. Martin thought he might be dealing with at least one of the above."

"What about lost or stolen?" I could still hope the paintings were the real thing, couldn't I?

"Sure, I deal with art theft too. But let's not play games here. If you want my help, you'd better give it to me straight."

I told him how Diane had left a watercolor of the lake with me and how I'd found what I'd thought was an authentic Georgia O'Keeffe oil hidden behind it, only to have it stolen from me.

"Red Canna? Cropped real tight? No background?" he asked.

"That's the one. How did you know that?"

"Somebody offered it for sale in New York this week, opened negotiations with a dealer here. Talkin' big bucks."

"How big?" I had to know what the painting was worth. Diane had turned it over to me, after all, told me to do anything I wanted with it. I had some pretty strong associations with that painting. I could even have gotten myself killed over it.

"Over a hundred thousand."

"A dealer would pay that?" I almost choked on the words. I'd loved that Red Canna. Why hadn't I hidden it more carefully?

"The dealer will try to negotiate down. All he's seen so far is a videotape. He won't commit until he sees the genuine article."

"Then he might buy it?"

"Right now, he's stalling. We want to catch these guys."

"Why did they go to a dealer?"

"Do you know how these things work? The dealer's the high priest of the art world. He buys the work, then sells it to a collector. Some dealers don't look too close. Fortunately, this guy looked close enough to smell a rat."

"A rat?"

"Forgery."

"Forgery? What made him think so?"

"Job makes him suspicious, same way mine makes me."

"Why couldn't the painting be authentic? O'Keeffe summered around here. Couldn't she have left paintings behind?"

"Not likely. Never heard of any."

"What if they were only found recently? Maybe been stored away in an attic or a closet all these years. That's possible, isn't it?"

"I wouldn't bet the farm on it if I were you."

"Didn't some of O'Keeffe's early watercolors turn up unexpectedly about ten years ago? Why couldn't that happen here?" I hated to give up the shred of hope

I had left.

"The ones that ended up in Kansas City in the Kemper Museum, you mean? Different scenario. And why are you saying they? You've seen others?"

"Look. I've stumbled on something very strange." I didn't know if I could trust him but I had to chance it. I described the hidden room and the flower paintings.

"Go on Tell me all of it," he said.

"I think Martin saw them too. Did he tell you he did?"

He hesitated again. "No. He hinted he had something important to discuss with me, but he never called back."

"I found a list of paintings in Martin's notes. I think it was a list of what he saw in that room. He got killed a short time afterward."

"How many paintings were there?"

"Twelve to fifteen, all flowers. They were everywhere -- on easels, leaning against the walls. Blew my mind. I never saw anything like it. The Red Canna we found at my friend's place had been covered by both the watercolor and a sheet but these weren't wrapped or covered or anything. Just spread out all around the room."

"Drying." He sounded annoyingly sure of himself.

"What?"

"Drying. An oil needs two years, sometimes longer than that even. They can't sell forgeries until they're thoroughly dry."

"Somebody else was with me when I saw the paintings -- a girl, sixteen years old. Now we can't locate her. I'm worried."

"You got reason to be. If the people involved in this con are the ones I suspect, they're a nasty bunch. What's the fastest way to get to where you are? Train?"

"Car. Got one?" I said.

"Sure. Sit tight 'til I get there. How long will it take me?"

"Four hours, give or take a little." I gave him directions to my place.

"Never mind that. Tell me how to get to where the paintings are," he said.

Now it was my turn to hesitate. What if he wasn't a detective? What if I was the one being conned? "Who'd you say you worked for?"

"Hey kiddo, you're in no position to be too fussy. But I'm legit. Don't worry about that part of it. Worry about your young friend."

I gave him directions to the Marlborough House Inn.

He didn't have to tell me to worry about Josie. The iceberg bobbing around in my insides could have starred in a Titanic movie. As soon as we hung up, I started calling everyone in the phone book named Harris. I'd run through five families before I got a nibble.

"Billy? You want Billy?" a child's voice asked. Then an ear piercing shriek, "Ma, where'd Billy go?"

I heard some muttering in the background.

"Not here. Might've gone to work," the child reported.

"Does he work at the Marlborough House?"

"Yeah, try there."

"But isn't the inn closed?" I started, but she'd already banged down the phone.

I had no better luck with Diane or Tom. I left messages for both of them to call me. I considered phoning Kevin, but why? Did I expect him to hold my hand, tell me not to worry? Joe Grazzia had me scared enough. I didn't need Kevin adding his two cents.

I called Kate. No answer either at the house or the restaurant. I hated leaving the message I left on her machine, but I had to do it. "Kate, I'm worried. If you haven't found Josie, call the sheriff and report her missing. Urgent. Get back to me and I'll explain."

I wandered through the camp, sifting through Joe Grazzia's remarks. Videotape? Somebody had videotaped the painting. I remembered the brightly lighted living room at Diane's summerhouse. The videotape could have been made right there. That would explain the unusual lighting. Then, before the taping was finished and the lights turned off, someone had been stabbed to death. Thieves fall out, the old saying went. But who were the thieves and why would they fall out after they had what they wanted? The money, probably. Maybe an argument over splitting the money.

My jacket was still lying on the chair where I'd left it. I picked it up and carried it to the window. I studied the slash of flame-red color on the sleeve. Up close, it didn't look so much like pizza sauce. The scene at the Marlborough House replayed itself in my head like my own personal videotape. Josie had startled me when she came through the closet. I'd jumped and hit one of the easels. As I turned to her, I'd reached out my hand to keep the easel from toppling over. I'd brushed against the canvas then, but which canvas? Josie had said something, something about seeing the oriental poppies on a postage stamp. That was the painting I'd rubbed against, I was sure of it. The stain on my jacket wasn't pizza sauce; the red-orange smudge was the exact color of O'Keeffe's poppies. The painting I'd brushed against had still been wet.

Joe Grazzia was right: the paintings were wet, at least one of them was. They hadn't been painted seventy years ago. I'd been reluctant to concede they were forgeries; I'd wanted so much for them to be the real thing. Maybe that was the reason some of the dealers didn't look too close, didn't check too carefully. Like me, they wanted to believe they'd found the real thing

Joe Grazzia had sounded annoyingly sure of himself -- but people could be annoyingly sure of themselves and still be right.

TWENTY-FIVE

So if forgery was the bottom line, who was the forger? The most likely candidate -- Edward Maranville. He was a painter in his own right, Diane had told me, as well as an expert on virtually every type of painting. His insistence that the Red Canna belonged to him began to make sense. Of course, it belonged to him if he'd painted it.

But it couldn't be that simple, could it? Edward had broken into my home, threatened me with a gun and demanded the painting, but I found it hard to believe he would have killed me to get it. I didn't see him having the guts for serious criminal activity. He'd need help. And, unless he was playing out some elaborate charade, Edward hadn't been the one who'd stolen the Red Canna from my uncle's camp and taken it to New York to sell. Someone else had to be involved in the con, someone shrewder and more ruthless than Edward, someone who'd literally stab a man in the back to get what he wanted.

Joe Grazzia had advised me to sit tight, but that

didn't mean I couldn't talk to Edward. I knew where he was after all -- the Tumbling Brook Motel. I'd agreed not to call the sheriff on him; maybe he'd return the favor by telling me if he had any idea what had happened to Josie.

I climbed into the van and headed north. First rain, then sleet pelted the windshield. Sheets of water swept across the road, leaving a thin layer of black ice behind. I missed the turn up the mountain and had to backtrack. The road was slick and treacherous; the woebegone brook that ran beside it, so plugged with dead leaves it didn't have a tumble left to its name.

The motel, a cluster of shabby brown log cabins, looked as if it had shut down for the season. The red Vacancy sign in the office was turned off; but I could see a faint light in a large cabin perched on the hill behind the others. The owners' place, I assumed. Perhaps they could tell me where Edward had gone. I shifted into low and forced the van up the rutted driveway. I was high on the side of the mountain now, looking down through the bare trees at the lake. As I approached the cabin, I spotted the roof of the Marlborough House off to my right, further north along the shore.

I knocked sharply on the door. Heavy drapes had been drawn across a picture window but I got a sense of someone inside. The door swung open slowly -- very slowly. Edward Maranville stood in the opening.

"How thoughtful, Ellen. You've come to check on me, to ascertain if I'm all right." He was wearing a dress shirt and tie, his suit jacket and coat were thrown across a chair behind him.

Edward's style of dress startled me, but not as much as the room. Heavy motel-type furniture had been pushed back to the walls to make space for a beige camelback sofa and a large club chair. The sofa and chair, along with a mahogany coffee table, were arranged on a magnificent Oriental rug, hardly the type of furnishings I'd expected to find at the Tumbling Brook. Through the open door to the bedroom I could see Edward's Louis Vitton luggage, still unpacked.

I stared at him, full of unspoken questions.

Edward gave an airy wave in the direction of the furniture. "Oh, I sent for a few of my things. The place was tres tacky. They laughingly call this the master suite, but you wouldn't believe the decor."

"But weren't the sheriff's deputies watching your house?"

"They were watching for something mundane -- my car in the drive, lights coming on inside the house. I sent a trucker under cover of daylight to go in the back door and bring me a few prized possessions I can't live without. No one even noticed."

"Why? Do you plan to stay here?" I asked.

"That wind is piercing. Let's not hold the door open. Come in." He looked past me down the dark driveway.

"I don't understand. Aren't you going back to your house?"

He shrugged. "Things have become more complicated than I like."

I didn't want to ask about Josie too quickly. If I could get him talking... "Edward, the painting you were looking for when you came to my uncle's, the Red Canna. Is it a fake?"

"A fake?" He motioned for me to sit on the couch and settled himself in the club chair opposite me. "A fake? Ellen, let me tell you something. There is no such thing as fake art. Many works of art are misattributed. Does that make them any less beautiful, any less pleasing to the eye, less satisfying to the soul?"

"Edward..."

"Fakes, as you call them, can give years of pleasure. They are things of beauty to be enjoyed for what they are, not for their signatures."

"But..."

"For example, do you know that one out of twenty van Goghs was not done by van Gogh himself but has been misattributed. What does that say about your experts? How much can they know when they can't identify what you call a fake?"

"I can't answer that question, Edward, but I want you to tell me the truth. Did you paint the Red Canna?"

"Yes, I've painted what you would call fakes, hundreds of them. I've done the works of Picasso, Modigliani, van Gogh, Degas, an occasional Vermeer, other old masters, impressionists, moderns. I've done them all. Perhaps you'll write an article about me some time. Make me as famous as de Hory or Van Meergen."

"Excuse me?" This man could lose me faster than anyone I'd ever met.

"They're famous for their fakes. There is a wonderful story about Van Meergen. He was a Dutchman, you know. Sold a painting to Goring during World War II. At the end of the war he was arrested for collaborating with the enemy, destined for a long prison term. He declared the work a forgery, admitted to painting it himself, got off with a much lighter sentence. Better to be a forger than a collaborator, you see."

I put my fingers between my teeth and whistled at him, a shrill, annoying blast of sound, then held out my hand for him to stop. "Edward, for God's sake, answer me, did you paint the Red Canna?"

"I can tell you now. It doesn't matter. Yes, I painted it. It's breathtaking, isn't it?"

It had taken my breath away, he was right about that. I nodded. "And did you do the Black Iris as well?"

"Black Iris III? O'Keeffe's favorite, it's been said. The perfect merging of botany and anatomy. Did you notice the richness, the depth of color? She could find the black iris only at certain New York florists for two weeks in the spring. Such a rare flower. Stieglitz saw her like that, you know."

For once I understood what he was talking about.

O'Keeffe had painted the iris; Stieglitz had photographed her as it embodiment, open, yielding, exquisitely sensual. "Actually Edward, I do know that. But right now, I'm trying to get something straight. Do you copy Georgia O'Keeffe's work?"

"Oh Ellen, my paintings are not copies. They're originals. I paint in the style of a certain artist. O'Keeffe often did a series of paintings, you know. Who can be sure how many? There are differences in all of them, sometimes subtle, sometimes more distinct."

"So buyers believe your flower paintings are part of her series?"

"O'Keeffe's flowers are a joy to do. No backgrounds, nothing to trip one up. Backgrounds can be treacherous, you know. Move an Oriental rug pattern into the wrong century and it will give you away faster than anything else."

Keeping Edward focused on what I wanted to know wasn't an easy task. "But you sell the works as O'Keeffe's, not as your own?"

"The experts have given me little choice. They crucified me when I did my own work, but they loved my fakes, as you term them. I could command sixty thousand dollars apiece for them, and that was years ago. Not as much as the originals would have fetched perhaps, but so many collectors wanted to own the art without the high price tag. The Texas oilionaires adored me. And they still do. No wonder. They love to walk their guests into their drawing rooms and show off their collections. What do the guests know? It's all the same to them."

"Edward, did Martin Cascadden know about your work?"

"He'd stumbled onto some of my paintings, I believe. Old Mr. Trevellyan showed them to him. Asked Martin what he made of them."

"And what did he make of them?"

"He assumed they were the lost O'Keeffe's people

talked about. Came to me and asked my opinion. Had no idea I was the one spreading the rumors about them."

"You, Edward? You spread those rumors?"

"There'd been speculation for years that O'Keeffe left paintings behind here. After the Ted Reid watercolors surfaced, the rumors seemed even more plausible. I simply mentioned them to a few people. A tactic to stimulate sales, give clients reason to think my paintings were authentic even when they suspected they couldn't be. People love to know and not know at the same time. Haven't you noticed that?"

"Did you tell Martin Cascadden you were the one who'd painted them?"

"Of course not."

The next question was a tough one, but I had to ask it. "Edward, was Martin Cascadden murdered? Did someone arrange his accident?"

"No. He was such a Nervous Nellie. The poor fellow was so excited about what he'd seen, his head was full of it. He drove himself in front of a truck. An unfortunate accident."

"Nothing more?"

"No one can say otherwise."

My own head was full too but I had to keep going. "Did you do all of the paintings, all the ones in the room at the Marlborough House?"

"So you've been snooping too, like Martin and your teenage friend. But it no longer matters. They're out of there by now. Yes, I did them all. O'Keeffes by EVM, you might call them."

"My teenage friend? Are you talking about Josie Donohue? Edward, that's really why I've come here. I have to find her."

"I suppose that's her name. Friend of the boy who works at the inn, she claimed, but she was poking around, inquisitive, nose in other people's business. Bertholdt hates that kind of thing."

"Has something happened to her? Where is she now?"

"Oh, she'll be all right. She's staying at the inn, under wraps, you might say." He uttered a thin, mirthless laugh. "She'll be all right if she cooperates."

Josie cooperating with Bertholdt? Not in this lifetime. "And if she doesn't?"

Edward shrugged. "The matter is out of my hands."

Suddenly, everything clicked into place: Edward's remarks about being able to tell me now, the admission that he was the forger -- although we'd both avoided using the word -- his unguarded comments, first about Martin and now about Josie. Edward was leaving. His overcoat and suit jacket were laid out on the chair. The suitcases I'd seen as unpacked were actually repacked and ready to go. I saw it clearly now. Someone -- probably Bertholdt -- would come with the paintings and pick him up and they'd be gone before morning, leaving Edward's precious furniture stored at the motel until he could send for it. Perhaps Bertholdt had already set out.

I jumped up. The rain beating on the roof sounded like a truck laboring up the drive, but I took time to ask one last question. "The man who was killed, Edward. Who was he? You must know."

"Never mind. I've told you enough."

I kept my face expressionless, my voice steady. I couldn't let him see how frightened I was. I was terrified now for Josie, convinced I had to get away and find her before Bertholdt found me there. "Edward, you've been very forthright. I didn't mean to pry. I'm simply trying to understand. Your work is exquisite, as good as O'Keeffe's certainly, perhaps better for all I know."

"Why didn't the critics see that?"

"I don't know why the critics didn't appreciate you. You're right, it doesn't seem fair." I edged toward the door.

"They've been hateful to me. I've tried to tell people that and they won't listen." He stood up and took a step toward me.

"Maybe I could do an article on you, make people see how unfair the critics have been. Not tell where you're living, of course, but talk about your talent, your versatility."

"Yes, we could do that. I'd want you to emphasize my talent, of course, but I'd like the critics to see that talent alone isn't enough. There's so much more I have to think about."

"Then, it's more than a matter of working -- how did you put it -- in the style of another painter?" Tell me quick, I wanted to shout. I had to get out of there and look for Josie.

"Of course. For example, do you think you walk into an art supply store and pick up authentic papers? No, the papers you use must date from the same time period as the originals. How many secondhand bookstores do you think I've gone through searching through antique books for end sheets suitable for my drawings? And the pigments, the frames. Do you have any idea how fortunate I was that Diane asked me to appraise those ugly old watercolors at her summerhouse? The very frames O'Keeffe might have used herself. Same age, same kind of wood. A dealer looks at things like that you know when he's establishing authenticity."

"Really? Diane's frames were what you wanted?"

"They were John's frames too. He let me have them. They were a real find, especially when I saw I could use the watercolors to hide the oils until time to sell them. Those frames worked well for me."

Edward was right. His story would make a terrific article, one I'd love to write some day. But I didn't have time for it now. I had to find Josie before something more happened to her. I inched closer to the door, relieved I hadn't taken off my coat, expecting Edward to realize how much he'd told me and stop me from leaving.

"Edward, keep thinking about what you'd want me to include in an article about you. Call me, we'll set up an appointment." I scribbled my telephone number on a scrap of paper and handed it to him. When he glanced down at it, I pulled the door open, ready to run if I had to. To my surprise, he let me go without protest.

TWENTY-SIX

Two minutes later I was hurtling down the mountain in the van, my body hunched forward over the steering wheel, my eyes straining to pick out the edges of the narrow road in the dark. If I could just get to the main highway without killing myself and without meeting another vehicle... I was convinced Bertholdt would soon be driving up this road and that, within a short time, Bertholdt, Edward and the paintings would disappear forever. But what about Josie? Would she disappear with them or would they find a way to silence her before they left? I began to shake uncontrollably. What if she was dead already?

As I neared the bottom of the hill, the van skidded on a patch of ice and almost went flying into a tree. My heart pounded; my hands on the wheel were slippery with sweat, but I knew what I had to do. In the seconds I'd stood on the top step outside Edward's cabin, I'd looked down at the huge bulk of the Marlborough House looming below me on the lakeshore to the north. I could see the inn clearly from that vantage point, outlined as if by moonlight -- but there was no moon. Lights, not very bright, but definitely outdoor lights, illuminated the south wall of the inn. The Marlborough House was closed. Why would someone have turned on the lights?

I watched for a place where I could call the sheriff, but the few businesses along the deserted highway were closed for the night. I scanned the sides of the road, hoping to spot an outside phone booth. Nothing. Maybe at the Marlborough House, I thought, maybe there'd be a way I could telephone from there. I felt as if hours had passed before I reached the road to the Anderson cottage. Rather than approach the inn head on, I turned in and took the shortcut through the trees. I switched off the headlights. The road dissolved into inky blackness. Trees pressed in on me like ghosts, fierce and menacing in the darkness. I rubbed my hands, one at a time, against my jeans, wiping my palms.

Suddenly, I was jolted forward, then thrown back against the seat as the van banged against an object I couldn't see, a rock or stump, maybe even a fallen tree. I'd hit something. Calm down, I told myself. You won't be any help to Josie if you kill yourself looking for her. But I couldn't calm down. I jumped out of the van and closed the door as quietly as I could. In the dim light I saw the outline of a car parked in the road ahead of the van. A few yards more and I would have crashed into it. A black Mercedes. I peered inside as I ran past it. It was empty.

Icy rain peppered my face. The wind tore at me, almost knocking me off my feet. I pulled up the hood of Ray's big coat, but I couldn't stop shivering. Twice I stumbled over roots; once I fell and landed hard, stunned but thankful I'd caught myself before my bad knee hit the ground.

When I could finally see into the cleared space around the Marlborough House, my suspicions were confirmed. A panel truck had been backed up to the inn's front door. Two lights placed in trees to accent the landscaping illuminated a small section of the Marlborough grounds, turning the truck a sickly yellow and casting an eerie glow over everything. As I huddled behind a tree, Billy Harris and a man I didn't recognize emerged from the front door carrying a flat wooden crate approximately three by four feet in size, a crate large enough to hold any of the paintings I'd seen in the hidden room.

As the men lifted the crate slowly into the truck, the wind caught it like a sail and flung it sideward, almost knocking it out of their hands.

"Careful. Damn it, don't drop it," someone said from inside the truck

The voice was muffled, but familiar, a voice I'd heard recently.

"Wait, wait. I can't get a good grip on it. Somebody get up here and help me."

The men on the ground lowered the crate. Billy Harris grabbed the edge of the opening and pulled himself up. The other man yanked his Coors cap down on his head and turned away from the wind. I slipped from the safety of the tree and ducked behind a privet hedge on the south side of a small garden, now reduced to lifeless stalks.

As the men busied themselves with the crate again, I sprinted around the front of the truck and crouched in the shadows on the far side. I crept closer and peered into the truck's dark interior. I had to know who was inside. My heart was thumping so loud I was sure everyone on this side of the lake could hear it.

The crate banged against the side of the truck. "What's with this wind anyway?" someone snarled.

The man inside the truck stepped forward. "Quick. Slide it in."

It was John Anderson.

While the men were pushing the crate toward him,

I seized my chance. Bent almost double, I dashed for the front door. I stopped just long enough to pull the M key off its hook behind the desk and headed for the stairs. The elevator door was open with another crate similar to the one that had just been loaded propped against the wall.

Enough adrenaline pumped through my body to send me full speed up the stairs to the top floor without a stop. Even my knee cooperated. I shoved open the door from the stairwell and peeked into the dark fourth floor corridor. The one faint path of light in the hallway came from the living room of the suite I'd let myself into a few days before. If only Josie was in there now. I tiptoed toward the open door, keeping close to the wall. The living room itself was in darkness but light shone from the closet. I crept up to it, looking for places to hide in case Billy and the trucker came back.

I took one step into the closet, then another. I could hear sounds of someone moving around in the interior room but I couldn't see anyone. I tiptoed further into the closet. I remembered the falling hanger the day I'd been there with Josie. I steadied the hangers on the clothes bar but I couldn't stop my own hands from shaking. Bertholdt stood in the middle of the room, making notations on the outside of a crate. I did a fast count; there were at least four other crates standing along the walls. One bit of luck anyway -- the men hadn't finished loading the truck yet.

I guess I was too far inside the closet to hear the elevator because the sounds of footsteps in the hall caught me by surprise. I barely had time to slip back into the living room and tuck myself behind the cherry highboy when the man I'd seen with Billy came into the room. Billy lagged behind him. He was shivering in spite of his heavy red plaid mackinaw and slapping his arms. Before he could follow the other man into the closet, I stepped out from behind the highboy tapping my finger against my lips in an exaggerated gesture for silence.

Billy turned ghostly pale when he saw me leap out of the shadows but, to my relief, he didn't utter a sound.

"Josie?" I whispered the word.

He stared at me, dumbfounded. For a minute I wondered if he could answer at all without her there to prompt him.

"Basement," he finally muttered, his voice very low, then added something that sounded like "me too." Before I could ask him to repeat the remark, an angry voice called to him through the closet door.

"Hurry up, kid. What's taking you so long?"

Billy threw me a frightened glance and hurried into the closet. As he bolted past me, I caught a whiff of his mac. The blend of wet wool and food smells, overlaid with perspiration and burning wood, was the same smell I'd noticed that Sunday afternoon in Diane's hallway. I was sure of it. Billy Harris was the person who'd been hiding at the Andersons' that day, the one who'd run down the stairs and shoved me. And here I was counting on him for help.

I got out of the suite fast and set a new record for a dash down four flights of stairs in the dark. The basement corridor was black as a tomb. Deep in the pocket of Ray's coat my fingers closed around the flashlight I'd used to look for my keys but I hesitated to turn it on. Instead, I felt my way along the wall toward the bar. I needed a plan and I needed it fast. I wanted to make a call to the sheriff but I had no idea where I'd find a phone on this level except in the bar and I doubted if even a master key would let me in there. If I could just find Josie... I'd start with the hideaway where we'd surprised Tom Durocher, then locate the storage room where Jack Whittemore had questioned Diane and me about the murder.

I turned on the flash for a second and flicked its beam over the nearest door. G-5 was imprinted there in small brass letters. As I stared at the number, I realized what Billy had said. G-2 -- ground, room number 2. I flashed the light on a door opposite. No number on that door or the one next to it, but I was sure I was on the right track. I'd almost reached the end of the corridor when I found what I was searching for -- G-2. I unlocked the door. The room was even darker than the hallway but I still hesitated to use the light.

"Josie, Josie," I whispered.

I heard a strange crackling sound, then an odd pop. "Josie."

More crackling. I turned on the flashlight, moving its beam slowly along the perimeter of the room.

Josie lay on the floor near the far wall, squinting against the light, her body wrapped tightly in ropes, her mouth taped shut with a wide strip of transparent wrapping tape. She was lying on a large, folded piece of bubble wrap that gave off the peculiar, crackling noise whenever she moved.

I rushed over to her and hugged her tight against me. I tried to ease the tape off her mouth. I knew it was going to hurt. She shook her head and looked pointedly at the ropes. I tugged at the cords that bound her hands, then loosened the ropes that held her arms tight to her body. As soon as her arms were free, she reached up and pulled the tape off her mouth herself.

"Son of a bitch. That hurt."

"Josie, are you all right. How long have you been tied up like this?"

"Days, I think. It's about time you got here."

"What?"

"Some partner you are. Hurry. Get those ropes off my legs. My feet feel like there's a million needles stuck into 'em."

I yanked on the rest of the ropes until she was free. I got an arm under her back and eased her into a sitting position. "Don't try to stand up yet. Rub your legs first."

"Got any food on you? I'm starving."

I dug through my pockets and handed her the tail end of a roll of mints.

She popped them into her mouth "We gotta get out of here. They come back to check on me every so often and they're about due."

"Who checks on you?"

"Bertholdt and a guy in a Coors hat. They let me go in that little john over there and use the toilet and get a drink. The Coors guy even brought me some food a couple of times. Not Bertholdt though. He's one mean hombre."

"Josie, what about Billy? Is he in on this? I know now he's the one who pushed me that day at Diane's."

"Yeah. He told me."

"What?"

"He made me promise not to tell you. He thought you'd already left so he came downstairs. He didn't mean for you to get hurt."

"But why was he upstairs? The place was on fire."

"The paintings, remember? He'd just brought one over from the inn, that one you guys found a few days later. It looked to him like the fire was out so he did what he was supposed to do -- put the painting upstairs in the closet. Bill's no rocket scientist, you know."

"You'll have to tell me more later. You're right about getting out of here. They're loading the paintings onto a truck and when they get done..."

I pulled Josie onto her feet. She was wobbly, but with my arm around her waist, she moved fairly well.

"I feel like I'm walking on hunks of wood, except those needles are more like splinters now. Man, they hurt," she said as we started down the corridor.

"Do you want to rest a minute?" I asked her.

"No. I just want to blow this place. Can we get through that door down there, do you think?"

Even in the low beam of the flashlight, I could see the heavy, steel door at the end of the hallway was chained and padlocked shut. I tightened my arm around her. “I’m afraid the lobby’s the only way out. I got in without anyone seeing me. We’ll have to try to get out the same way.

TWENTY-SEVEN

The door to the stairway creaked as I wrenched it open, a loud scraping sound that reverberated through the quiet dark. I froze. Nothing moved. I reached behind me for Josie's hand and dragged her after me up the stairs. She was so stiff she could hardly lift her feet from one step to the next. She made low groaning sounds deep in her throat but she kept moving. At the first floor landing I cracked the door and surveyed the dimly lit lobby. The elevator door was closed now. The room was empty. The white phone on the registration desk looked tantalizingly close.

"Josie, can you run," I whispered.

"I can sure as hell try," she said in my ear.

"Let's get behind the desk."

We scuttled across the room and crawled under the counter. I reached for the phone and brought it down on the floor next to me. I lifted the receiver and pushed 9-1-1. The beeps as I hit each number sounded like a string of firecrackers going off.

I'd whispered the words "sheriff" and

"Marlborough House" when I heard an angry voice from outside. John Anderson's voice.

"What was that? Somebody said something."

"Nah, it's the wind," another voice assured him.

The wind was roaring off the lake in gusts, blasting through the open door and across the floor. I shoved the receiver inside my coat, hoping to muffle the 9-1-1 operator's response, and peered out the door. I could see the truck still backed up to the building. Shadowy forms moved around inside. The wind whipped the treetops into a frenzy of motion. The bushes by the inn's front entrance were flattened almost to the ground.

"I heard somebody, I tell you. Where's Bertholdt?" John Anderson said.

I flattened myself against the baseboard just as John climbed down from the truck and stomped into the lobby. As soon as he passed me, I slithered back under the desk.

As if on cue, the elevator door opened. I recognized Bertholdt's low-pitched growl. "This is the last crate. We're ready to leave."

"You're picking up Edward?" John asked.

"Of course, Edward goes with me. He had no right to let you represent him, John, I've told you that. Edward and I have been together too long for him to make changes at this stage of the game."

"And my commissions?"

"From sales to your clients? I'll be sending those to you as agreed."

I wondered if that promise sounded as phony to John Anderson as it did to me.

"And what will you do about the girl?" John asked.

Josie squeezed my arm.

"Leave her right where she is, the little snoop," Bertholdt snarled.

"You can't. The inn's closed. She could die down there."

Josie tightened her pressure on my arm. At least John cared what happened to her.

"So, she'll die. Charles died. You weren't quite so concerned about him."

"That was an accident. You know I never meant..."

"Never meant to kill him, John? Try that one on a jury."

Josie's plopped her hand over her mouth to cut off her surprised gasp. I bit down hard on my bottom lip.

"Bertholdt, I know this girl. I can't let her die down there."

"And I knew Charles. How do you think I felt about him? You care about that girl, you go untie her." Bertholdt's voice was laden with contempt, any pretense at friendliness gone.

"Look, you know I can't. If I do, she'll realize I'm involved in this."

"You're the big shot CPA, John. Think of something."

A rough voice interrupted them. "Knock it off, you guys. The truck's ready to go. I'll check the girl for you. Then Nate and I are out of here."

I heard the door to the stairwell open and the clump of someone's feet on the stairs. Then, other footsteps. Through a little crack in the desk, I saw two pairs of wing tips moving toward the front door.

As soon as they disappeared, I pulled the receiver out of my coat. I tried to get the operator again, but there was no one on the line. I hung up and whispered to Josie, "That guy checking on you will tell them you're gone. We've got to make a run for it."

"So let's do it," she said.

"Don't stop for anything. If they catch one of us, the other keeps going to get help," I told her.

"Gotcha," Josie said, pressing against me.

I reached behind me and seized her hand, then crossed my fingers with a desperate wish we could get out without anyone noticing us. We slipped through the door and sidled down the far edge of the steps into a driving rainstorm. I could barely make out the shadowy forms of John and Bertholdt moving away from us toward the Mercedes. We were almost in the clear when the phone rang.

"Oh no. That's the callback from 9-1-1. I forgot they do that," Josie whispered.

John and Bertholdt swung around, puzzled at the sound.

A big, ugly looking guy materialized at the open front door of the inn. "Hey, wait a minute, you two. The girl's gone. She's not down there," he shouted

Bertholdt and John hesitated, then turned back toward the inn. Bertholdt saw us and pointed. "There she is. Go after her. Don't let her get away."

The man vaulted off the steps, light as a gymnast despite his bulk, and hit the ground running only a few yards behind us. He was the kind of guy you have nightmares about -- huge, burly, a dark watch cap pulled low over a face contorted with rage. We tore across the inn's side yard, heading toward a stand of trees, cut off from the place where my van was parked. I stole a quick glance over my shoulder as John and Bertholdt joined our pursuer. Behind us I heard an angry exchange, garbled but clear enough for me to recognize some choice obscenities. The beam from a large flashlight swept over us.

The rain blew off the lake in torrents, stabbing into my eyes, burning like fire. I could hear the crash of water against the rocks, pounding as loud as ocean surf. My heart thudded even louder than the water. I dug deep into the pocket of Ray's coat for my own flashlight. My hand slid over something else, something I'd forgotten was still in there. I felt the hard, smooth barrel of Edward's gun.

Josie pulled up beside me, pointing downhill toward the lake. Miraculously, she seemed to know where we were. We thrashed through piles of leaves so wet and slippery I had trouble staying on my feet. Muttered curses from behind us told me the men weren't finding the ground any easier to navigate than I was. With Josie leading the way, we zigzagged around a clump of shrubs and through a thin line of spindly plantings, a boundary of some kind.

"Hearthstone. Campsites," she squeaked.

Once past the fringe of trees we struck bare ground. She pointed left and we ran through the ruts of a dirt road that led up toward the highway. The campground was deserted, shut down for the winter. Picnic tables were stacked one on top of another along the road. Stone fireplaces loomed among the trees like phantoms in the mist.

The road climbed steeply uphill. We were both fighting for breath, slowing down more than I liked. I chanced another look behind me to see how fast the men were gaining on us. The trucker was loping along like a marathoner. John and Bertholdt, both of them surprisingly fast on their feet, hung in close behind him. Before I could turn my head away, the beam from the big flash caught me across the eyes. Suddenly I couldn't see anything ahead of me but an exploding flare of light. Blinded, I staggered off the road and into a pile of firewood. As I pitched forward, struggling to right myself, the pile collapsed under my weight, sending logs rolling in all directions.

"Keep going," I yelled to Josie. I shoved at the cascading hunks of wood, caught in a mini-landslide, tossed about like one of the logs. Something came down hard on my head and shoulders as I twisted my body around, trying to get my feet onto something solid. The man in the watch cap let out a roar and bore down on me. He beamed the flashlight full on me as I lay flat on my back in the middle of the scattered logs. Bertholdt and John pulled up beside him.

I flailed my arms and legs around, powerless to get up or even turn over, flipped like a turtle at the mercy of its predators. I couldn't make my legs work. I reached into my pocket. My fingers closed around the butt of Edward's gun. I breathed a prayer of thanks that I'd worn Ray's coat.

I lifted the gun and pointed it from one man to the other. "Get away. I'm not afraid to use this."

John stepped back and the man in the watch cap followed his lead. Bertholdt held his ground and stared at me. The light from the flash glittered along the gun barrel.

"Who the hell are you?" Bertholdt snarled.

"Go on. Move away. All we want to do is get out of here." I levered myself up on one elbow. I put both hands on the gun and shoved it out in front of me, taking aim.

Bertholdt jumped in surprise but he stayed where he was. His voice grew thicker and more guttural. "Well, Ms. Busybody, I don't think that's possible. Put down that gun before somebody gets hurt."

"I mean it. Get away." My own voice sounded equally tough and mean -- at least I hoped it did -- but my insides had turned to mush.

Bertholdt's spewed out something in a language I didn't recognize but he didn't back off. He inched toward me one step at a time, as if hoping I wouldn't notice. Suddenly, with a huge shout, Josie came barreling down the hill out of the mist and crashed into him from the side. He let out a grunt of surprise and flung her off. She crumpled into a heap on the ground a few feet away from him. He reached for a thick hunk of wood and advanced on her.

"You little bitch. We should have got rid of you two days ago." He raised the log over his head.

I didn't want to shoot anyone, really I didn't, but I couldn't let him hit Josie with that log. I aimed for Bertholdt's legs. Fortunately, they were as thick as the fireplaces so they were hard to miss. I fired and heard the thwack of the bullet hitting his thigh.

He dropped the log and grabbed for his leg. "You shot me. Damn you to hell," he said, turning toward me.

I pushed myself up higher on my elbows and held the gun out in front of me, ready to fire again if I had to.

Josie sat up, shaking her head admiringly. "Cool, El. I didn't know you were packin.'"

John and the trucker melted into the trees. "Bertholdt, come on. Let's get the hell out of here before she kills one of us," John said.

But Bertholdt's rage wouldn't let him retreat. He limped toward me, his face twisted into a mask of pain and fury. "I'll kill you for that," he screamed, lunging at me.

I wrenched my upper body sideways as far as I could. I ducked my head and fired again. Bertholdt careened past me just as the campsite exploded with light. Sheriff's cars pulled up to the entrance gate, facing the barricade, shining their headlights down the hill. The flashing red lights turned the mist, trees and muddy terrain into an alien landscape. Bertholdt wheeled and galloped stiff-legged back toward the Marlborough House. Uniformed deputies rushed toward us, slipping and sliding along the wet ground. Billy Harris raced beside them, motioning for them to hurry.

"Are you all right? Stay where you are for now," one of the deputies called as he and the others disappeared into the woods.

I was twisting from side to side, trying to get up when Kevin Mulvaney knelt down next to me.

"Ellen, how do you get yourself into these messes?" His words sounded a bit too sharp for the circumstances, I thought, but his hands were gentle as he pushed me down against a log and felt along my arms and legs. "Do you think you've got broken bones?"

"No, but I can't seem to move my legs," I said.

Josie walked slowly toward us, rubbing her cheek. "That guy really hit hard. He would of croaked me, if Ellen hadn't shot him."

"Ellen, I don't believe this. You shot somebody?" Kevin said.

"Help me up. Pull me onto my feet so I can get out of here." I tried again to stand on my own, but I couldn't do it.

Kevin slipped his arm around my shoulders. "Stay right there. Don't even try to stand up."

I let him take charge. For once I didn't mind him telling me what to do. I heard him shouting that he needed an ambulance, watched without protest as he took off his coat and tucked it around me. I felt as if everything was happening at a great distance. He knelt down on the ground next to me and took hold of my hand. I clung to his hand as I drifted in and out of unconsciousness. I came awake just as he unclasped my fingers and stood up. Rain was streaming off his hair and face; his shirt was soaked. He signaled toward the top of the hill where an ambulance had pulled up near the barricade.

All the doors of the ambulance opened at once as the rescue squad members jumped out and started down the hill. In seconds Mike, an EMT I knew from Kate's restaurant, reached my side. He waved to two of his companions to bring a stretcher. "Ms. Davies, is it really you? Don't worry. We're going to take care of you."

I didn't feel any pain as Mike poked and prodded me. I drifted off again, rousing only long enough to see the deputies herding John Anderson up the hill toward one of the sheriff's cars. After a time I felt myself being lifted onto the stretcher. I must have been delirious by then because I thought I saw Kevin put his arms around Josie and pull her close and I thought Josie -- instead of belting him -- leaned her head gratefully against him. And I must have been hearing things too –

because I swore Billy Harris ran up to us, talking a blue streak, explaining how he'd searched the inn for Josie but couldn't rescue her with the rest of the gang watching him.

The next thing I remembered I was lying in the ambulance with Josie sitting next to me as we sped down the Bolton Road and onto the Northway above Lake George Village. I kept trying to tell Josie to watch for a yellow truck and a black Mercedes, but I couldn't make her hear me over the shriek of the siren.

Josie hovered above me, slicking my wet hair off my face again and again. "Don't die on me, El. Please, don't die on me."

I hadn't thought I was hurt bad enough to die, but she looked mighty worried.

TWENTY-EIGHT

I woke sometime during the night to the gray shadows of a hospital room. I sifted through jumbled recollections -- the speeding ambulance, the glaring lights of the emergency room, a cold table in X-ray and finally the long, bumpy ride through a warren of empty corridors to a clean, dry bed. Josie had stayed beside me the entire time, even when other faces and voices crowded in -- nurses and doctors, Kevin, Jack Whittemore, and later, Kate and Diane.

I was alone in the dark. My head ached and one side of it felt tender to the touch. I located an egg-sized bump near my right ear but I couldn't feel any bandages. My left arm had been immobilized somehow and I couldn't reach my right hand down far enough to feel my legs. I was swaddled in a rigid cocoon. I tried to kick off the covers but they were tucked under the mattress so tight I couldn't move them. I concentrated all my willpower and slid my legs a few inches back and forth, thankful to find them working again.

A figure stretched out in a reclining chair across

the room stirred, then got up and came toward me. Kevin leaned over the bed. "Ellen, are you awake?"

"Never mind awake. Am I alive?" I asked.

"You were banged up pretty bad, but you'll be all right. You have a concussion and a nasty break in your left arm. It's in a cast. Your legs seem to be all right. Are you in pain?"

"I don't think so. What about Josie?"

"Bruised, but otherwise okay. Scared to death you were going to die on her. Kate finally pried her away from you about an hour ago and talked her into going home."

"What about...?" I realized the words I muttered were unintelligible. I let them drift away and slipped back into sleep.

Daylight showed beneath the window shades the next time I woke. A pretty little girl in a brown and yellow uniform plopped a tray on my bedside table. "Breakfast," she said cheerfully as she went out.

I could smell coffee; I could see a pot of it on the tray. I was desperate for that coffee but I couldn't reach it. I looked around the room. The other bed and the recliner were both empty. Where was that Kevin when I needed him?

Apparently, all I had to do was form the question in my mind because the next thing I knew he was standing beside the bed. He had the crumpled look you expect in a guy who's spent the night in a chair but he'd managed a shave and his hair was freshly combed. He looked good to me, really good.

"Coffee," I said, pointing at the tray.

"Ellen, Jack Whittemore's out there with another man, a detective who says he spoke to you on the phone. He's going back to New York this morning and would like to see you before he leaves."

"Coffee," I said again.

Kevin filled a cup from the pot and held it to my lips. "I don't think you're able to talk to anybody."

I took a sip of the coffee. "Help me get this down and I will be."

A nurse bustled in. "Visitors here to see you. Much too early for them, but they've got the right credentials."

As soon as I drained the cup, she rolled up my bed and ran water in the sink. She soaked a washcloth in hot water and handed it to me. "You'll feel better if you wash your face. Do you want me to comb your hair?"

I nodded. I didn't think I could raise my hand far enough to do it myself.

Kevin was helping me slurp up a second cup of coffee when Jack Whittemore marched into the room. The man who followed him was almost a foot shorter than Jack and at least a hundred pounds lighter. His long, dirty-looking dark hair and heavy black beard were a perfect accompaniment to his frayed jeans and leather jacket. I wished Josie could have met him; she would have loved his earring.

My welcoming smile didn't come off so well, I guess, because Jack turned quickly to Kevin. "Is she all right?"

I was interested in that information myself. I knew Kevin had explained my injuries to me at some point during the night, but I had only the foggiest memory of what he'd said.

He recapped for Jack in his usual concise manner. "Broken arm, concussion, several bad contusions. Twisted ankle, painful but not broken."

"What's with the bruise on her face. One of those guys hit her?" Jack asked.

Kevin took away the cup and leaned down to me. "Ellen, how much do you remember? Did someone hit you?"

"Logs. Logs hit me. Did you stop the truck?" My voice sounded weak, a sick person's voice.

"Truck was found abandoned early this morning outside of Albany. We've seized the paintings but the driver got away. The others, too," Jack Whittemore said.

I cleared my throat and spoke up as loud as I could. "Bertholdt and Edward might not have been in the truck. Bertholdt could have been driving a black Mercedes. Did you know that?" I asked.

"Yeah, Billy Harris told us eventually. We alerted the State Police but they never spotted it. They may have hidden that vehicle somewhere and switched cars. Those guys are no amateurs, remember."

"You can say that again," I said, shuddering.

"Josie Donohue insists you saved her life, Ms. Davies. I'd like to hear more about what happened. I understand you used an unregistered weapon to shoot her assailant?"

"I used Edward Maranville's gun. I had to do it. Bertholdt was going to kill Josie." I was glad I'd thought to use the word kill. It sounded much more serious than hit or club. Was I in big trouble over the gun? I couldn't think about it right then. I was too sleepy.

I'd started to close my eyes when the man next to Jack leaned across the bed and stuck out his hand. He looked more like an artist than a detective, but I guess that was the point. "Joe Grazzia. I thought you were going to wait for me."

I liked his style. I might be banged up but I could still shake hands. "I was too worried about the friend I mentioned to wait for you. When I heard her mother hadn't seen her in two days, I thought she'd gone to the Marlborough House. I was afraid she was going to be killed."

Jack Whittemore cut in. "So you took it on yourself to go after her. You seem to have an affinity for murder, Ms. Davies. Last night you were lucky it wasn't your own."

"I know. I know," I said. I didn't have enough energy to argue that point.

"You might also like to know we've arrested John Anderson. He's confessed to killing Bertholdt Ulrich's partner, Charles Renault," Whittemore said.

"Yes, I heard John admit he killed him," I said.

"What? You knew that?" Jack Whittemore was not pleased.

"I made my explanation short and quick. "I overheard him talking about it at the Marlborough House. He said it was an accident."

"That's his story. Says he and Edward were videotaping a painting when Bertholdt and Charles burst in on them. They got into a nasty argument. John picked up a letter opener, claims he was waving it around to protect himself when Renault rushed him and it caught him in the worst possible spot. It's not easy to kill someone like that, especially when you only stab him once, but Anderson hit a vital spot."

"John Anderson a murderer. I can't believe it," I said.

Whittemore continued. "If he gets himself a good enough lawyer, a jury may decide it was self defense. No witnesses, at least right now. But he's facing other charges as well, including an arson charge. When Ulrich and Maranville left him holding the bag, he set his own place on fire to hide the evidence."

"You mean John set the fire at the summerhouse himself?" I wondered how Diane had reacted to that piece of news. John would be safer in jail for a while.

"That's what he told us," Whittemore said. "Arson isn't a new crime around the lake. One of Anderson's clients lost his restaurant that way a few years ago. John might have picked up the idea from him. Just didn't pay enough attention to how to pull it off successfully."

"So if John's in jail and the others are gone, who gets the paintings?" I said.

"Grazzia here wants to take 'em back to New York with him. He plans to catch up with those two characters eventually. I guess our department doesn't have any problem with that."

"And Edward? What will happen to him now?" I asked. I might have been conning Edward at first with my talk of writing an article about him, but the more I thought about it... He'd make a fascinating subject, no doubt about that.

Joe Grazzia leaned in closer to me. "Ms. Davies, let me give you a few high points here and then I'll get out of your hair. Maranville's real name is Edouard de Villemarin. He's a well-known character in the art world. Tried to retire about ten years ago when he moved to Glens Falls but art is his great love and he can't stay away from it. When he runs low on money, he succumbs to temptation and whips off a few forgeries. Usually starts with drawings. He can do one of them in a few hours, but he likes the challenge of oils and the oils sell for a heck of a lot more."

"And John Anderson was part of this con? Why? He's a successful CPA. Why would he jeopardize his reputation that way?" I said.

"He told Jack here he didn't know it was a con in the beginning. Maranville, as you folks know him, came to him for help in selling off his family's art collection. Romanian aristocrats, he called them. He's used that line before and people always fall for it. Anderson suspected he'd come into the art fraudulently, thought maybe he'd got hold of some of the stuff the Nazis confiscated during World War II. Maranville wasn't doing the O'Keeffe knock-offs at that point – he was pushing European painters then – but Anderson suspected something fishy because no matter how high a commission he charged, Maranville never objected."

"When did he find out the paintings were forgeries?" Kevin asked.

Whittemore fielded that question. "Maybe a year or so ago when Maranville couldn't produce one. Anderson had it sold to a collector he knew in Chicago and the guy was getting antsy. John kept nagging Maranville about it until he finally admitted it wasn't dry."

"And that's the way John found out?" Kevin said.

Joe Grazzia winked at me. "Told you drying was a problem, kiddo. The ones you saw at the Marlborough House weren't dry either, you know. When the gang realized they had to hit the road, they didn't dare put the watercolors into the frames on top of the oils. They had no choice but to crate 'em up as carefully as they could and move 'em just as they were."

"But I found a second painting in Diane's closet, do you know that? It was a Black Iris without a watercolor over it. How did that get there?"

"A mix-up, I guess. The kid helping them just took whatever he found in a certain spot, didn't ask any questions. Probably knew they'd stopped covering them and thought he was supposed to move that one over to the Andersons' like he'd done with the Red Canna. We're trying to find out exactly how many others he moved over there, but the kid's hard to pin down."

Josie could find out easy enough. She'd love to be called in on the case, but I wasn't about to say so. Anyway, I was still puzzling over John Anderson and his role in all this. "So John Anderson went along with this whole scheme, even after he knew the truth? I don't understand it."

For once Jack Whittemore actually agreed with me. "You're right. That's a tough one to figure. We think he was in too deep to get out. The fees he'd been charging really amounted to blackmail -- all of 'em knew that. And Anderson had an expensive courtship going with that rich broad he'd taken up with."

"But what role did Bertholdt and Charles play in all this?" I said.

Grazzia took up the story again. "Former partners of Maranville's. He could do the art but he was no good at selling his forgeries. Those two did it for him. When they found out John was horning in on the business, they started coming here to the lake to make sure they got their cut."

"But if Bertholdt knew John had killed Charles Renault, why didn't he turn him in for it?" I asked him.

"Couldn't call attention to himself and the scam. Agencies in several countries are looking for him. The only thing on his mind that night was to get out of there. He grabbed the painting and the videotape they were making of it and high-tailed it back to the Marlborough House, left Maranville and Anderson to fend for themselves. Jack can tell you what happened then," Grazzia said.

Jack was glad to oblige. "As Grazzia here said, those guys were paying young Billy Harris to take the paintings over to the Anderson place one at a time as soon as they were dry enough to be fitted with the watercolors. Apparently, Bertholdt brought the painting back to the inn late that Saturday night and put the watercolor into the frame right away to hide the oil. Bill came to work the next day, saw the painting and carried it over to the Andersons' like he thought he was supposed to do. He told us he smelled smoke and saw the mess on the living room floor but the fire seemed to have gone out. His orders had been to get the paintings into the closet and not let anyone see him doing it. He was almost home free when you and Mrs. Anderson came in and found the body. So he finished up his part of the job even though he had to knock you around to do it. But Bertholdt didn't dare go to the Anderson place and retrieve the Red Canna until we got through investigating. By that time Diane had brought it to you."

"Do you think Bertholdt's the one who took the Red Canna from my uncle's?" A wave of fear and nausea washed over me. What if I'd been home when he came after it? If I'd found Bertholdt in my kitchen instead of Edward, I'd probably be dead right now.

"That's the way we figure it," Whittemore said. "He

must have found out some way or other that Diane had brought it to your place. Then he waited until you went out, broke in and took it. Maranville was hiding out but he'd traced it to you too. He was probably scared of what Bertholdt might do, thought he might blame him for the mess because he was the one who'd gotten them involved with Anderson."

"And he was probably right about that," Grazzia said. "Bertholdt had a ferocious temper. Mean enough to kill anyone who crossed him. John Anderson was lucky he got out of this mess alive. And I might mention that certain others were too."

I flashed on Bertholdt's arm raising the hunk of wood as he bore down on Josie and me, his features contorted with rage. "I know, I know," I said.

Even in my weakened condition, I could see Whittemore and Kevin cranking up to belabor that point, so I changed the subject fast. "When Diane and I saw Bertholdt at the Marlborough House the day we found the body, he did a great job of acting really surprised about the murder," I said.

"I doubt he was acting. He didn't expect people to think the body was Edward's," Whittemore said.

It was too much for me to sort through. "So, now you've got the flower paintings but Bertholdt's got Edward. Is Edward in danger?" I asked.

Grazzia shrugged. "Probably not as long as he stays a good meal ticket. The two of them will surface again. We'll get another crack at these guys soon or later."

I thought of a dozen more questions but my eyes kept closing and I couldn't find the words I wanted.

Joe Grazzia smiled sympathetically. "Listen, kiddo, I gotta split. You know my number. Call me when you feel better," he said.

I managed a little wave as he and Jack left.

Kevin took off a short time later. "I'll shower and change and come right back. You had a tough night. Take a nap, why don't you," he said as he went out.

A nap sounded good. I deserved it.

Edward Maranville was gone, I told myself as I settled down to sleep. So were the flower paintings and my idea for an article on Edward that would have shaken the art world to the core. But all wasn't lost. Edward had provided me with a great hook for my O'Keeffe feature and a thousand unanswered questions to ponder. As for Whittemore's crack about my affinity for murder, I wasn't planning to ponder that remark at all. For all I knew, maybe murder had an affinity for me. And I really didn't want to think about that either.

Two days later when Kevin brought me home from the hospital, I was feeling almost like my old self. He settled me in, then checked my cupboards and rushed off to do grocery shopping for me. I was alone when Diane Anderson tapped on the kitchen door.

"Brought you something," she said as she came in.

"You've brought me half a dozen gifts in the last two days. Enough already."

"This one's the best. You'll like it." She reached back outside the door and set the Black Iris III on the floor in front of me.

"No way," I said.

"A loaner. Temporary at best. I told Joe Grazzia we still had one painting left at our summerhouse and to tell me the best way to send it to him. He acted as if he didn't care. So, here. Keep it until he asks for it."

"Oh no. Been there, done that," I said.

"Ellen, you love these flower paintings. Why not enjoy this one for a while, just 'til Grazzia wants it?"

As we all know, the flesh is weak. At least mine had proven to be — especially where those erotic flowers were concerned. I loved that painting as much or more than the Red Canna, so I accepted the loan. A few days later when my uncle drove down from Hague to check on my injuries, I got his permission to redecorate the living room. As soon as I could bumble along with my one good arm, Josie and I painted the walls white like

O'Keeffe's walls at Abiquiu and replaced Mattie's old fashioned tieback curtains with shutters.

Kevin insisted it would be a terrible mistake to paint the fireplace bricks white, but the Black Iris got to him too (with a little help from me, of course) and he did it anyway. When I added my new white slipcovers, the room looked crisp and stark, like something O'Keeffe would have designed for herself. The focal point, of course, was the Black Iris III hanging over the white fireplace. Guests were always taken aback by it. I loved to watch their mouths drop open when they saw how stunningly beautiful it was, loved to watch them realize it was an oil, not a poster or a print. A few people even had the nerve to ask me how I came by it. But I soon discovered if I smiled enigmatically and didn't answer, they never asked again. People love to know and not know at the same time. Edward was right about that.

ABOUT THE AUTHOR

Anne White has been a life-long writer, editor and librarian. Her articles and short stories have been published in McCall's magazine, Career World magazine, Lake George Arts Project Literary Review, and Glen Falls Post Star, and among other publications. She holds a Master's Degree in Library and Information Science and a Bachelor of Arts, cum laude, in English.

Affinity for Murder is White's first novel. Her second in the Lake George Mystery Series, Arranging the Pieces, is slated to be forthcoming from Oak Tree Press, and she has the third novel in progress.

Anne White makes her home in Glen Falls, NY.

ABOUT THE ARTIST

Mary Montague Sikes (Monti to her friends) has studied with such famed artists as Peter Saul and Diana Kurz, Jim La France and Elaine Harvey. Her art has been exhibited at Roanoke Museum of Fine Art, Virginia Museum of Fine Arts, Johns Hopkins University and Piedmont Arts Center, and other fine galleries.

In addition to this novel, Monti has provided the cover art for several Oak Tree books, including her own Hearts Across Forever, due in July 2001. Her art-and-narrative high concept large format book, Hotels to Remember is set for a Spring 2001 release.

More Dark Oak Mysteries you will enjoy...

Callie & the Dealer & a Dog Named Jake
by Wendy Howell Mills

Callie, a restaurateur on North Carolina's Outer Banks, has problems. Someone is stealing from the storeroom, her past is haunting her and a hurricane is blowing in...but things really get interesting when she funds a dead man in her freezer.

ISBN 1-892343-15-0 $8.95

By Letha Albright

Reporter Viv Powers confronts the challenge of her life when her love, Charley, is accused of murder and will do nothing to defend himself — not even declare his innocence to her. A firm believer in logic and facts, Viv learns to face the trials of faith as she pursues the truth and the reasons why Charley isn't talking.

ISBN 1-892343-12-6 $7.95

Available at Barnes & Noble and other fine bookstores, Amazon.com and other internet booksellers, or direct from the publisher.

Dark Oak 2001 Mystery Contest

Grand Prize Winner to be announced in
Fall 2001.

~

Visit our website at www.oaktreebooks.com for information on the winners, guidelines for the upcoming Dark Oak 2002, and details on our other fine books.

~

Oak Tree Press books are available at Barnes & Noble and other fine bookstores, Amazon.com and other internet booksellers, or direct from the publisher.

~

For more information, send SASE to:

Oak Tree Press
915 W. Foothill Blvd. #411
Claremont, CA 91711-3356
909/625-8400 Tel 909/624-3930